"What are you doing, Dillon?" Tannis asked in a voice that trembled with panic and excitement.

"Something I've been wanting to do since you first walked into my office," he said. "Something that's been pretty near impossible until now." He pulled away the pieces of her disguise and wiped away the smudged makeup. "There now, that's better," he said, his thumb skimming lightly across her lower lip. "Now . . ." he said breathlessly before pulling her into his arms.

It was just as she'd thought it would be— a plunge from the high board, dizzying, exhilarating . . . terrifying. She felt as if she were falling, and clutched at Dillon for support.

His arms gentled around her, his mouth softened, and his tongue traced and caressed her lips. He cradled her against him, stroked her body while he tasted her soft skin. He didn't only claim her mouth, he took possession of her entire body. It wasn't just a kiss, but a kind of erotic dance, something primitive and mysterious, that filled her head with thunder and her body with heat. . .

WHAT ARE *LOVESWEPT* ROMANCES?

They are stories of true romance and touching emotion. We believe those two very important ingredients are constants in our highly sensual and very believable stories in the *LOVESWEPT* line. Our goal is to give you, the reader, stories of consistently high quality that may sometimes make you laugh, sometimes make you cry, but are always fresh and creative and contain many delightful surprises within their pages.

Most romance fans read an enormous number of books. Those they truly love, they keep. Others may be traded with friends and soon forgotten. We hope that each *LOVESWEPT* romance will be a treasure—a "keeper." We will always try to publish

LOVE STORIES YOU'LL NEVER FORGET
BY AUTHORS YOU'LL ALWAYS REMEMBER

The Editors

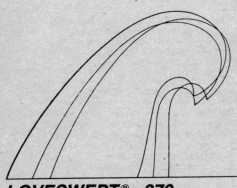

LOVESWEPT® • 279

Kathleen Creighton
Winter's Daughter

BANTAM BOOKS
TORONTO • NEW YORK • LONDON • SYDNEY • AUCKLAND

WINTER'S DAUGHTER
A Bantam Book / September 1988

If you would be interested in receiving protective vinyl
covers for your Loveswept books, please write to this address
for information:

Loveswept
Bantam Books
P.O. Box 985
Hicksville, NY 11802

ISBN 0-553-21924-3

Published simultaneously in the United States and Canada

PRINTED IN THE UNITED STATES OF AMERICA

O   0 9 8 7 6 5 4 3 2 1

For Laura,
in celebration of spring!

One

The January sunrise touched the derelict with gentle fingers, warming him. He stirred, scratched himself, then took a small flat bottle from inside his jacket. Painstakingly he unscrewed the cap and filled his mouth with amber liquid. While he was rolling it around on his tongue, he splashed some onto the lapels of his coat, and more onto the dirty sweatshirt underneath. Then, with a furtive glance around him, he leaned over and spat the whiskey from his mouth onto the grass.

As he was tucking the bottle into his coat, he noticed a bag lady coming along the concrete walkway, pushing her shopping cart. The early morning sun was at her back, glinting off the metal cart and throwing an elongated shadow ahead of her onto the path. Over wisps of nondescript hair she wore a purple knit cap: a ski cap, the kind with a big, fuzzy pompon on the top. The derelict settled his shoulders more comfortably against the side of a concrete planter filled with pungent pink, white, and purple stock and watched the pompon's shadow bob toward him. He wondered how long the woman had been on the streets; he hadn't seen her around the park before.

"Good mornin' to you." The shadow had draped itself

across his legs and stopped there. The derelict thumbed back the brim of his filthy baseball cap and squinted up at the bag lady.

She was smiling at him. Her face was weathered and wrinkled, but her eyes were the clearest, bluest blue he'd ever seen, minute reflections of the winter sky. Something went *clunk* inside him; he felt an odd sense of recognition, as if he ought to know her, somehow. He could see that she had once been beautiful. He wondered if, in a younger, happier incarnation, her face might have graced his boyhood fantasies, those endless Saturday afternoons in darkened movie theaters. . . .

Unexpectedly charmed, the derelict muttered, "Good morning," and lurched to his feet.

"My name's Win," the bag lady said, leaning across her cart to offer him a hand clad in a ratty brown wool glove. As he took the hand, the derelict saw the blue eyes cloud over. Small wonder, he thought, she'd probably gotten a whiff of the booze.

But the look on the bag lady's face was one of compassion, not disgust. From somewhere in the depths of her shopping cart she produced an orange, which she pressed into his hands. "Have some breakfast," she said. "You'll feel better." She smiled at him and started on her way.

"Wait," the derelict said, reluctant to lose her company. He felt as if he'd spotted a precious jewel glittering in shifting sands; if he didn't grasp it now, it would be lost forever.

The bag lady paused and turned, her brows raised expectantly. Impulsively the derelict leaned down and plucked a sprig of lavender stock from the flower bed. "Here," he said gruffly as he handed it to her. "For the breakfast."

Her smile became radiant. The derelict heard a little catch in her breathing as, murmuring thanks, she wove the flower's stem into the knit cap, just above her left ear. And then, with a wave of her gloved hand, she went shuffling off down the path.

Dillon James watched her go, absently turning the orange over and over in his hand. Under the bill of his old Dodger cap his eyes were narrowed with the complexity of his thoughts. It had been a long time since he'd been on the streets, and his cop sense was pretty rusty. Rusty, but not dead. He'd been touched by the woman's act of kindness and knocked out by her inherent charm, but now that she'd gone and taken that potent charisma with her, every instinct and sixth sense he'd ever had was screaming at him. His scalp was prickling. He had that old, familiar creepy feeling, as if something alive and probably carnivorous were crawling down his spine.

Whoever she was, that bag lady just didn't track.

Methodically, following half-forgotten procedures, he went over a mental checklist beginning with the woman's appearance: Clothes—that purple knit cap, a long wool coat of some indeterminate tweed that looked as if it had once been expensive—probably from a charity box or thrift store. Run-down shoes a few sizes too big for her; she'd padded them with several pairs of socks but still walked with an awkward, sliding shuffle. Nothing out of the ordinary about any of that. The cap and gloves were a little warm for southern California, maybe, but on the other hand, the nights could get chilly in January here on the edge of the Mojave Desert.

It bothered him that he couldn't determine her age. The limp, graying hair meant nothing. Some people grayed early, and poverty had a way of speeding up the process. The lines in her face could be the result of exposure to sun and wind and the dry desert air, elements that wouldn't affect the clear blue of her eyes or the whiteness of her teeth. There had been a certain puffiness in her cheeks, but it was hard to tell, with the coat buttoned to her chin, whether her bulkiness was fat or just layers of clothing.

All in all, Dillon thought, her appearance, the shuffling walk, the overburdened cart, all seemed right on target. No different from any of the hundreds of homeless people he'd come in contact with during his years as a vice cop in downtown L.A. Her appearance was right. It was her manner that was wrong. She was too open, too friendly, too trusting. Everything about her looks indicated she'd been on the streets for a long time. So where was the defensive posture, the glare of suspicion and hostility? Without a good, healthy dose of paranoia, no one, man or woman, would survive long on the streets.

For the benefit of anyone who might have been watching, Dillon dropped the orange into his coat pocket and stood for a moment or two, swaying, blinking, absently scratching. Then, with one hand placed protectively over the bottle in his coat pocket, he shuffled off after the bag lady.

He didn't know who she was, or why she'd made such an impression on him. He just had this feeling she needed protecting, somehow. He'd sensed a kind of innocence about her, a childlike naïveté that both charmed and angered him. For God's sake, didn't she know the streets were a jungle? There were wolves out there . . . and nobody knew that better than Dillon James.

"Oh . . . shoot!"

Muttering under her breath, Tannis Winter braced herself and managed to wrestle the teetering shopping cart down off the curb. A bus that was just pulling away from the stop honked at her, then roared on by, belching clouds of diesel fumes in her face. Ignoring the bus, Tannis wedged the cart's wheels against the curb and bent over to retrieve the items that had fallen off into the gutter: a rolled-up newspaper yellowed from lying unclaimed on someone's front lawn; a brown paper bag containing a bunch of wilted carrots and some brownish bananas; a pair of child's tennis shoes tied together by the laces.

All the items were precious to her. The newspaper would be handy for sitting on when the grass was wet or the sidewalk grimy. The groceries were from her friend Binnie, who worried about whether Tannis was getting enough vegetables and always shared her gleanings from the trash bins behind the Food Fair market over on Pacific Street. The shoes were practically brand new and had once belonged to Tannis's five-year-old nephew, Joshua. His mother, Tannis's sister Lisa, had a tendency to buy things just the right size, forgetting how rapidly small boys grow. Which was all right with Tannis. She knew she would find a good home for those shoes. . . .

Something winked at her from the gutter filth, something shiny and metallic, spotlighted by the morning sun. Investigation unearthed unexpected treasure—a quarter. Tannis happily picked it up and tucked it away in the handbag she wore hidden inside her voluminous coat. Her delight in the serendipitous discovery was tempered by concern; someone had obviously dropped part of his bus fare. She hoped whoever it was hadn't been too badly inconvenienced. She especially hoped it hadn't been a child.

The quarter wasn't the only treasure Tannis found at that bus stop. A few feet away from the quarter she found a perfectly good pencil, and, beyond that, a flattened soft drink can and nearly half a pack of cigarettes. She tossed the cigarettes back into the gutter— she had no use for them since she didn't smoke—but the pencil went into her purse along with the quarter, and the can joined her collection in a plastic trash bag in the shopping cart. She could get cash for them at the recycling center. Pleased and cheered by the modest windfall, she straightened, tugged the cart around, and prepared to cross the street.

A hand at her coat sleeve arrested her. Startled, she turned and, in an unconscious, almost reflexive gesture, lifted her hand to touch the flower in her hat. "Oh," she said, smiling, "hello again."

It was the derelict from the park. She hadn't noticed before how tall and thin he was. As he stood in the street blocking her way, he seemed to sway like a tree in the wind. The initial rush of pleasure she'd felt on seeing him again faded; suddenly, and for no reason she could name, Tannis felt stirrings of unease. She told herself that he was harmless, that he was only drunk, poor man. Much more drunk than she'd thought, obviously; more drunk than he'd seemed when he'd given her the flower.

The derelict swayed toward her, loomed over her. Standing in his shadow, she felt chilled and uncertain. She was suddenly very conscious of the hand on her arm; brown, long-fingered, and very strong, the wrist sinewy as rawhide. It occurred to her that the dirty brown jacket that hung from those broad, raw-boned shoulders must conceal a body that was just as strong, just as supple, just as hard. She didn't know how she knew; there was just something about the lines of his body that reminded her of a cocked bow.

"Hey," the man said softly in his cracked and ruined voice, "you dropped something." He held up the pack of cigarettes she'd just discarded, waving it between two long fingers. He was smiling, but it seemed to Tannis that there was something almost wolfish, now, about the way his teeth gleamed in his hollow-cheeked, dark-stubbled face.

"Those aren't—ain't mine," she rasped, suddenly remembering to disguise her voice. Jerking her arm from the man's grasp, she hunched her shoulders and pushed on her cart with all her might, sending it rattling and clanking across the pavement.

As she crossed the street, a new and unfamiliar fear pursued her, so potent it felt like a tangible thing, like a dog, snarling and snapping at her heels. Finally safe on the other side, she turned and looked back. The derelict was still standing where she'd left him. And suddenly she felt ashamed.

How could she have treated him so rudely? He'd only tried to be friendly, and after all, wasn't that what she was here for? To make friends with the street people, to understand them, to find out who they were and how they'd come to this?

And yet . . . Something deep inside her, something vulnerable and uniquely feminine understood instinctively that *this* man was different. There was something about him, something that set him apart from the other homeless people she'd befriended—people like Binnie, The Showman, Crazy Frankie, and poor sad, hopeless Clarence. And because she was a psychologist, she even understood that the differentness she found frightening now was the very thing she'd found so compelling about him in the first place. It was something intangible, something not even a quarter inch of dark stubble, a drunken slouch, and an aura of cheap booze could hide. Because, incredibly, in spite of all those things, the man was attractive.

He was attractive the way a predator is attractive, Tannis thought. The wolf, the leopard, and the hawk . . . and a certain kind of man—the type with quiet, watchful eyes, and a cruel twist to his sensual lips; the one with a body like a bullwhip, full of leashed power and sinuous grace. The kind of man who calls to something wild and primitive in a woman's soul, even though she knows he spells Danger with a capital D.

Small wonder, then, that when he had called to her there in the park the wild and primitive side of her had responded automatically, instinctively. And small wonder that those same instincts were warning her now of the danger.

But there was something else too. In the park she'd had the impression that she'd taken him by surprise, caught him in an unguarded moment—rather like coming upon a tiger asleep with his paws in the air. His spontaneous gesture of giving her the flower had been so endearingly charming, it had taken her breath away.

Just now, though, when he'd placed his hand on her arm, he'd seemed harder, darker, more alert, more focused. Focused on her. The tiger awake. And for some reason he'd followed her. His intense interest was enough to send a shiver of fear down her spine, but it had also occurred to her that he must have seen her pick up the quarter. She knew full well that street people had been murdered for the shoes on their feet, let alone money.

People had been telling her all along that she was crazy, that there was danger in what she was doing. Now, for the first time, Tannis knew they were right.

With her heart pounding and cold sweat trickling down her ribs, she hoisted the shopping cart over the curb on the far side of the street. After a moment's indecision she headed south, toward Cleveland Street. The derelict had followed her; possibly he was still following her, and there was no way she could outrun him or give him the slip without abandoning her cart. But she had friends on Cleveland Street. The butcher at Sam's Deli had given her scraps of cold cuts and had even let her use the bathroom once. And, of course, there was Gunner, the handicapped man who ran the newsstand on the corner. If there was anyone she could count on to help her, it was Gunner.

Dillon stared after the bulky, shuffling figure and looked thoughtfully at the cigarettes he still held in his hand. It was another incongruity, her passing up a good clean pack like that. Even if she didn't smoke, most of the street people he knew would consider them as good as money in trade. If she hadn't figured that out yet, she hadn't been on the streets very long. And yet, the cart and the clothes said otherwise. Odd.

Stuffing the cigarettes into his pocket, Dillon rubbed his hand across his mouth, waited for a break in traffic, and crossed the street. On the other side he paused, then turned south. His loose-jointed stride was deceptive; it looked aimless and unhurried but wasn't. In no time at all he had the bag lady's purple knit cap in sight again.

No doubt about it, he thought, there was something haywire about that woman. Here it was, a gorgeous January day, with clear skies and the mercury moving toward a high in the upper seventies, and she was still wearing the coat, cap, and gloves. Moving along as fast as she was and pushing that cart to boot, she had to be working up a sweat. Dillon was beginning to feel sticky himself, and all he had on under the jacket was a sweatshirt with the sleeves cut off and a pair of his oldest, rattiest jeans. He was beginning to itch too; the jacket's former occupant had had company.

He was getting too old for this, Dillon decided, indulging in a good scratch while his quarry waited fretfully at a stoplight. It had been a long time since he'd done any of this undercover stuff. Like his instincts, the old moves were coming back to him, and he hadn't lost much in the way of reflexes. He just didn't remember minding the discomforts so much.

Of course, he'd been a lot younger then. Younger, and idealistic enough to think he could make a difference. In the old days he'd known the seamy underside of the city as well as most people know their own living rooms. And he'd known the people—the hookers, the pimps, the winos and wierdos, the bag ladies, runaways, addicts and dealers—better than most people know their kids. Eventually, though, he'd gotten to feeling like the Dutch boy with his finger in the dike, and the time had come when he'd known he had to get out or wind up being sucked into the sewer himself.

• • •

The newsstand was closed. It was past ten o'clock. Tannis had forgotten Gunner's habit of slipping away to the deli for coffee and a bagel once the morning rush was over. She should have remembered. Sometimes, if her timing was right, she could get Gunner to bring back a cup of coffee for her, balancing it in the caddy he'd rigged up on the arm of his wheelchair.

As she leaned against the side of the newsstand to catch her breath, Tannis stole a quick look back. Yes, the wino was still coming, still following her, only half a block away now. He was impossible to miss—the blue baseball cap easily topped every other head in the crowd.

With a dry mouth and pounding heart she hurriedly looked around her, studying the lay of things, considering her options. About a block away she saw a police black-and-white rolling slowly toward her. Briefly she considered flagging it down but rejected that except as a last resort. It would surely mean questions and explanations, and the odds were that before she was through, her cover would be completely blown. Word traveled fast on the street. There had to be a better way of attracting the patrolmen's attention, one that wouldn't focus it needlessly on her.

"Hey!"

Tannis jumped as if she'd been stung as a dark, saturnine face was thrust around the corner of the newsstand, practically at her shoulder.

"Hey," the wino said, "where you goin' in such a hurry, huh?"

Tannis ducked her head, tucking her chin into the collar of her coat as she pushed away from the plywood wall. "I'm not goin' anywhere," she muttered, and added with one eye on the advancing patrol car, "I'm waitin' for a friend."

"I'll be your friend," the wino said in his soft, whis-key voice.

Tannis's breath caught. Her heartbeat accelerated as

she looked up into the derelict's face. *Friend?* It didn't seem likely; there was something dark about that face, something dark and dangerous.

A small movement drew her eyes downward. Deep in his coat pocket the wino's hand was turning the orange over and over, almost, she thought, as if he were caressing it. Oh, dear, Tannis thought, bitterly regretting the impulse that had led her to give it to him. Now what had she done? How in the world was she going to shake this poor guy? She didn't really want to hurt his feelings, but she couldn't have him following her around either. There was just something about him that unnerved her.

Out of the corner of her eye Tannis saw the patrol car cruise closer—only ten or fifteen yards away. She sucked in air. It was now or never.

"I have to go," she gasped, and aiming the cart at the derelict's midsection, she gave it a mighty shove. It caught him just below the place where his belt would have been if he'd been wearing a belt.

Air exploded from the wino's lungs. Hurtling backward in a half crouch, he struck a trash can a glancing blow. There was the sound of breaking glass. The trash can careened into the gutter and overturned, followed immediately by the wino, who landed on his backside squarely in the middle of a pile of spilled refuse.

Tannis clamped her hand over her mouth and stared in horror at the wino's contorted face. Well, she hadn't meant to hit him *there.* Too late for regrets though. It hadn't been pretty, and she wasn't proud of herself, but the maneuver had provided her chance to escape. As she was pushing her cart hurriedly down the sidewalk, she heard a screech that could only be the police car braking to a stop at the curb.

Dillon heard the screech too. It was followed by the slam of two car doors almost simultaneously. He heard a voice say disgustedly, "Jeez, Louise, ten o'clock in the morning. Isn't it a little early for this?"

Another voice answered, "Five'll get you ten he doesn't know what the hell time of day it is." Two pairs of khaki-clad legs planted themselves, one on each side of Dillon. The second voice went on, jacked up a notch or two now in volume. "Okay, buddy, having a little trouble keeping our feet, are we?"

Dillon just shook his head. He was getting his wind and probably even his voice back, but he didn't waste either one on explanations. It wasn't going to do him any good—these guys weren't about to believe him. Hell, he thought morosely, *I* wouldn't believe me.

One of the cops squatted down beside him and picked up a fragment of the broken whiskey bottle. "Whoo-whee!" he said, waving his hand in front of his nose. He glanced up at his partner. "Couldn't have wasted very much of this stuff, by the smell of him."

Dillon groaned and closed his eyes. "Hey, guys, this isn't what it looks like."

"Yeah?" The cop seemed interested. "What does it look like?"

Knowing it was pointless, Dillon said, "I know you think I'm drunk, but I'm not."

"Of course not," the squatting cop said in a soothing tone, "you're just a little under the weather, right?"

"More than a little, actually," Dillon muttered darkly. "Listen, I know you're not going to believe this, but I haven't drunk a drop of what was in that bottle."

"Right." The cop ducked his head to hide a grin. "Uh . . . you got any identification?"

Dillon just sighed and shook his head.

"Come on, buddy," the cop said, slipping a hand under Dillon's elbow. "I think you'd better come with us."

"What charge?" Dillon grunted as he was hoisted to his feet. And then, sourly, he said, "Never mind. Let me guess. Public intoxication? Disorderly conduct? Creating a public nuisance?"

The older of the two cops, the one who'd remained

standing, gave a low whistle and drawled, "You *are* familiar with the drill, aren't you? Been here a few times, I'll bet. So you know how it goes, right, my friend? You come along nicely, and you get to spend a couple days indoors, maybe dry out a little, get a couple square meals, compliments of the city of Los Padres. How's that sound?"

"Great," Dillon said, straightening and stretching experimentally, and discovering that the damage done to his anatomy by the shopping cart probably wasn't permanent. "Just . . . *great.*"

Resigned to the hassle, the inevitable indignities he knew he'd have to suffer before this whole mess was straightened out, Dillon settled into the back of the patrol car. He wasn't really thinking about his own situation at all. He was thinking about that woman, wondering who she was and what she was doing on the streets. Because for darn sure she wasn't any ordinary bag lady. Those eyes of hers . . . the clearest, bluest eyes he'd ever seen. Fire and ice. Looking into them had made him feel as if he'd just swallowed a hefty slug of pure white lightning. Maybe she was somebody he ought to recognize, and maybe she wasn't, but there was one thing he knew for sure: He'd know her if he ever saw her again. He'd know those eyes.

As the patrol car pulled away from the curb, Dillon turned to look back down the street. He didn't see any sign of the bag lady, but it didn't matter; he knew he'd be seeing her again, and a lot sooner than she thought if he had any of his old skills left at all. He was going to be looking for that woman, whoever she was and whatever her game was. And he'd find her too.

With a laugh that was more pained than amused he realized that he owed her one for what she'd done to him with that shopping cart.

"Lord, I hate this," the younger cop grumbled as he picked up the radio's hand unit, wrinkling his nose fastidiously.

The veteran gave his partner a look that was part amused, part cynical, and maybe a little sad. "Get used to it, kid."

Dillon knew exactly how he felt. He'd felt that way often enough himself.

He had no rancor for the two cops, even though they'd put a temporary crimp in his program. He just hoped Logan didn't come down too hard on them, that's all. Dillon was fairly certain the fertilizer was going to hit the fan when Los Padres's finest discovered that the wino they'd busted was their own newly elected city councilman.

Two

It was a long way from downtown Los Padres to the northern outskirts of the city, the area known as The Estates. It was certainly a long walk, especially pushing an overburdened shopping cart, but Tannis was always more conscious of an even greater distance that couldn't be measured in miles.

The Estates was a gated community bordering on the Los Padres Golf Course, home of the Los Padres Open, which only last year had become an official stop on the PGA tour. The homes were large, all built in the same Spanish style with red tile roofs and courtyards. The houses eventually gave way to pricey town house and condo complexes that clung to brush-covered hills overlooking the golf course. The streets of the neighborhood were broad and clean and sun-drenched. The air smelled of flowers and new-cut grass and, day or night, it seemed almost to breathe with the muted hiss of sprinklers.

As Tannis turned into Fountain Court, a short cul-de-sac backing onto the seventh fairway, she reached under her coat, opened her purse, and took out a small rectangular object. Taking aim at a sloping driveway occupied by a child's overturned tricycle, she pressed a button with her thumb, then waited while the massive garage door creaked slowly open.

Her aching muscles complained as she pushed the cart up the driveway and into the garage. Sweat itched and trickled under her arms, down her back, and in the hollow between her breasts. A shower was going to feel so good.

As the door clunked softly shut behind her, Tannis pushed the cart toward the far corner of the garage, maneuvering between a white BMW and a yellow Honda scooter. In the stuffy semi-darkness she pulled off the brown gloves, and then, with a grateful sigh, the purple knit cap and a lank, gray-streaked wig. Her fingers touched the cool petals of the flower woven into the cap, and she paused, frowning, while a little whirlwind of troubling feelings twisted and turned inside her. And then she tossed the cap into the shopping cart, closed her eyes, and indulged in a vigorous massage of her scalp, combing and fluffing her dark blond hair, reveling in the coolness of drying perspiration.

The door to the house opened, and a small woman with short blond hair and a worried crease between her eyes peered into the gloom. "Tan? Oh, good, it is you. What are you doing home? I thought you were going to be staying in town all week."

"Was," Tannis answered, shrugging out of the coat and placing it carefully across the top of the cart. Methodically she continued removing layers of shabby, shapeless clothing. "Changed my mind." And then, realizing she was still speaking in the gruff phrases she affected on the streets, she cleared her throat and gave a short laugh. "I couldn't stand it anymore, Lisa. You wouldn't believe how much I'm longing for a shower!"

"Oh, I believe it," her sister said pointedly, wrinkling her nose and watching with a mixture of distaste and awe as Tannis removed the pads from the insides of her cheeks and peeled bits of latex from her eyelids, nose, and chin. "Isn't it kind of cheating though?"

"What do you mean?" Stripped to her panties and bra, Tannis stepped out of the heavy, oversized shoes, then bent over to peel off three layers of mismatched socks. Holding them fastidiously by thumbs and forefingers, she dropped them on top of the mountain of clothing that had grown atop the shopping cart. Feeling lighter by about a thousand pounds, she closed her eyes, lifted her arms high, and dropped her head back, letting her hair swing free across her shoulder blades. "Oh *Lord*, how marvelous that feels!"

With curiosity rather than judgment in her tone, Lisa said, "Isn't it a little like putting on a blindfold to see what it's like to be blind? Or sitting in a wheelchair to feel what it must be like to be paralyzed? I mean, you know you can always take off the blindfold or get up out of the chair."

"It isn't the same thing," Tannis said, frowning. "I'm not doing this to see what it's like. I'm doing it to find out what *they're* like." She jerked her head toward the kitchen. "Uh . . . who's in there? Is it okay if I—"

"It's just me and Josh. Parade on through." Lisa swung the door open for her. "Richard's flight got grounded in Boston. He won't be back until this weekend at the earliest."

Tannis poked her head cautiously into the kitchen. Her nephew was sitting on the kitchen table, swinging his feet. His small shoulders were hunched, and there were suspicious smears across both cheeks.

"Hi, Josh," she said softly. "What's the matter?"

The little boy's expression was woebegone but stoic. He straightened his shoulders gamely, gave a prolonged sniff, and said dolefully, "Oh, I just fell off my bike. I skinned my knee, see?" he held it up for her inspection.

"Ouch," Tannis said, impressed. "That smarts. Oh, well, some Mercurochrome will make it feel better."

"And a Band-Aid," Josh said firmly. The deal had obviously already been struck.

"And a *kiss*." Tannis planted a noisy one on her nephew's smudged cheek and got a gratified sniff in response. "Better now?"

Josh nodded. She ruffled his hair and went on through the sprawling house to her room.

As she stripped off her bra and panties and stepped into the shower, she was frowning. It *wasn't* the same thing, she told herself, but what her sister had said bothered her anyway. Even though her reasons for doing what she was doing might be different, it was true that she *could* take off the blindfold whenever the going got too tough. She *could* jump from the wheelchair on two good legs if her life and health were at risk. She'd been living on the streets for weeks; she almost felt like one of them now—the legions of the lost, the faceless, the homeless, the ones who'd somehow slipped through the cracks of a system that prided itself on its benevolence.

But she wasn't really one of them. When she got cold or hungry, she could go home.

Or frightened. Even with hot water sluicing over her body, her skin still prickled and tingled with a rush of gooseflesh. That wino she'd met today . . . She'd thought about it all the way home, and she still didn't know what it was about him that was so . . . different. Partly, she knew, it was the man's eyes. Most of the time they had been in shadow, but the one clear glimpse she'd had of them, there beside Gunner's newsstand, had completely unnerved her. There had been intelligence there, and complete awareness. The man had acted drunk, but his eyes hadn't looked drunk. One could be faked; the other couldn't. Why had he pretended to be drunk when he wasn't? It was a puzzle.

When Tannis finally emerged from the bathroom, she found her sister sitting on the bed, scraping at her nails with an emery board and frowning.

"Josh is watching *Sesame Street*," Lisa said, tossing the nail file into the drawer of the bedside table and dusting her hands. "While we have some privacy, I want you to tell me what's wrong."

"What makes you think something's wrong?" Despite her denial, Tannis knew perfectly well it was pointless. Lisa was nothing if not tenacious.

Sure enough, the little crease between her sister's eyes deepened. "Why did you decide to come home?"

Tannis bent forward at the waist, toweling her hair. "Nothing's wrong," she said as she rubbed with unnecessary vigor at her scalp. "I told you—I just got tired of being itchy and filthy—"

"Bull pucky," her sister said primly.

"Bull *what*?" Laughing, Tannis straightened to give her trim, fastidious, suburban-housewife and perfect-mother sister a look of astonishment. Lisa returned it with one of complete aplomb. Still chuckling, Tannis said, "Look, Lisa, I know you always think—"

"And I'm always right, aren't I? I always know when something's bothering you that you don't want anyone to know about. Remember the time you got in trouble at school for putting chocolate milk in a water pistol and shooting the substitute teacher with it? And then you forged the note from Mom to the principal, telling him she couldn't come to the conference because she was in the hospital having her appendix out?"

"There's a lot to be said," Tannis remarked darkly, "for being an only child."

"Yeah, well, there's a lot to be said for brothers and sisters too. How about that big kid from . . . I forget—Chicago, or someplace, who decided to collect a toll in the rest room? You were afraid to tell anyone, but I got it out of you and told Mike and Jerry. Didn't you love the look on that girl's face when all four of us showed up in the girl's bathroom? And remember the time in eighth grade, when you were stringing those two guys along because you couldn't decide which one you liked best, and it was eating you alive . . . remember?"

"I remember," Tannis said softly.

"I got that out of you too," Lisa said.

"And didn't tell anyone." Tannis sighed and closed her eyes. "All right, so I'm . . . a little rattled, I guess. Something happened today. Something that . . . kind of scared me."

"More than 'kind of,' I'd say," Lisa murmured. "So what was it?"

Tannis threw her a frustrated look and picked up a hairbrush. She shrugged. "Oh, nothing really important, just this wino followed me, and then tried to waylay me. No big deal. I handled it okay. In fact—" She paused to smile grimly. "The last I saw of him, he was being hauled off by two cops in a patrol car."

"Doesn't sound like anything you haven't had to deal with before," Lisa said, the little crease of concern hovering. "Nothing your self-defense classes haven't prepared you for. And if the guy's been arrested—"

"I *know.*" Tannis dropped the brush onto the table-top and turned to face her sister. "I know. There was just something about this guy that . . . got to me." She doubled one hand into a fist and pressed it against the towel, just under her breasts. "I felt it—in *here.* And it's funny, because at first, when I saw him, there was something about him that really attracted me. I even gave him an orange, and then he gave me a flower." She touched her hair and smiled, remembering. "And then"—she hugged herself and shrugged—"I don't know what happened. All of a sudden I just . . . wanted to run away."

"Understandable," Lisa said dryly. "I'd want to run away all the time if I were doing what you're doing, living on the street, with those—" She broke off, shuddering.

"But that's just it, Lisa; I've never been afraid on the streets before. I don't think I realized, when I decided to do this for my doctoral project, that I was going to find such . . . rapport with those people. For one thing, they're not 'those people'—not anymore. One thing I found out right away was how little difference there is between most of them and any one of us."

"There but for the grace of God . . . ?"

"Exactly. They're people just like you and me, but they've had a little bad luck. For some of them, having no money, no job, and no home is the problem; for others it's just a symptom of the problem. And for a few, it's a way of life. Those are the ones that really fascinate me, they're the ones I want to do my study on—the ones who live on the streets because they choose to, for whatever reasons. The ones who actually prefer it to living in permanent homes."

Her voice had deepened, gone husky with emotion the way it always did when she talked about things that interested her. It had that passionate intensity most of the time, she realized, simply because she was interested in nearly everything.

"I want to know *why*, what makes them tick. And I need more time, dammit. I can't afford to come running home just because some . . . *bum* gives me a bad case of the jitters!"

"So you're going back?"

"Yes," Tannis said firmly. "Tomorrow."

"Well," Lisa said, getting up with a sigh, "I suppose you have to. I know nothing I or anybody else can say is going to stop you. But at least you know this guy's in jail."

"Dillon, for cryin' out loud, what are you trying to do to me?"

Dillon nursed one eye open and squinted up at the Los Padres chief of police. He muttered sourly, "Took you long enough. Where the hell have you been?"

There was a dangerous light in Logan Russell's eyes.

"I was in Santa Monica," he said with exaggerated precision, showing his teeth, "at a meeting with the President's Task Force on organized crime. Naturally when they yanked me out of a roomful of the top names in law enforcement in the entire *state* to tell me two of my own officers had just arrested a skid-row bum claiming to be my best friend, the newly elected city councilman, Dillon James, I just dropped everything to come a-running!" His voice, mild to begin with, had escalated to a roar that was only partly mitigated by a strong New Orleans accent.

When Logan paused, swearing, to drag a hand through his thinning blond hair, Dillon asked incredulously, "And you believed a story like that?"

Logan gave a disgusted snort. "It sounded like something you'd do." He stood aside and gestured for the uniformed guard beside him to open the cell—reluctantly, Dillon thought.

"You know, Logan, this is all your fault," he said as he slipped through the gate.

Logan jerked his head back as if something unpleasant had hit him in the face. "My Lord—what have you been wallowing in?"

"About a pint of cheap whiskey. Listen, if you hadn't talked me into coming back here and running for public office after I got out of law school—"

"So what is this, some kind of sick revenge?" The question was tossed back over a linebacker-broad shoulder as they hurried through the squad room under the interested scrutiny of half the law enforcement personnel of Los Padres. Pausing before his office door, Logan cast a nervous look around and dropped his voice to a raspy whisper. "Dillon, if this leaks, if the papers get hold of this, Flintridge will have my ass in a basket!"

Dillon chuckled as the door clicked shut behind him, then said placidly, "Don't worry about the mayor, I'll handle him."

"Yeah? You gonna 'handle' this too?" The police chief

reached for a sheet of paper and shot it across his desk at Dillon, missing him by a mile. Dillon snagged it and sat down in a chair to read it, ignoring Logan's pained look at the state of his clothes.

After a moment he swore softly and tossed the memo back on Logan's desk. "You've got to be kidding."

"Nope. Already under way." Logan sat on one corner of his desk and crossed his arms on a torso only slightly thicker than when it had filled out an LSU football jersey.

Dillon sat forward. "Logan, you know this isn't the answer."

There was a moment of silence, during which Logan looked harassed. He took a deep breath and exhaled it audibly through his nose. "You know it and I know it, and so do my people. But dammit, Dillon, I haven't got any choice. The statutes are on the books. Flintridge is within his authority as mayor of this town to demand that they be enforced."

"Damn!"

"Well, you can't blame the man. He's embarrassed. Can't you see the headline? CRUSADING COUNCIL-MAN ARRESTED ON SKID ROW! It's the kind of thing the wire services just love, you know that. This town has been working hard to attract the big-money tourist—move over Palm Springs. This kind of thing is a little rough on the image, know what I mean? Flintridge would much rather look at a headline that reads CRU-SADING MAYOR ORDERS SWEEP OF DOWNTOWN STREETS . . . VOWS TO CLEAN UP SKID ROW."

Dillon slapped his forehead. "What are you going to do with 'em all, Logan? It's January. They come from everywhere this time of year, looking for someplace to sleep where they won't freeze to death before they wake up. There's hundreds of them out there. The available shelters won't begin to hold them. There just isn't enough money in the city budget to put 'em up, not even for a few days, and the private agencies are already overwhelmed. What are you going to do with them?"

"You mean, what are *you* gonna do with 'em, Councilman James. That's your problem, not mine. My job is to follow orders and clear 'em off the street."

"They'll all be back in a few days, a couple weeks. You know that."

Logan nodded. "I do know that, yes. Unless, of course, you come up with a solution to the problems of mankind in the meantime?"

Dillon muttered bitterly under his breath.

Logan slipped off his desk and moved around it to his chair. "Dillon," he said in a kindly tone, "do me a favor, would you? Forget it for tonight. There's nothing you can do about it anyway. Go home. Take a bath. You smell like a latrine."

"Thanks," Dillon said sourly. Gingerly he pulled out the front of his sweatshirt with a thumb and forefinger, sniffed, coughed, and got to his feet.

"Don't mention it," the chief of police said cheerfully. "If you feel like it later, after you've had a bath, come over for a beer. Meredith and the kids'd love to see you."

"Thanks," Dillon said. "Maybe I will."

On the way down the backstairs of City Hall, he remembered that he'd intended to ask Logan for a make on his "bag lady." Hearing about the mayor's streetcleaning operation had driven that incident right out of his mind. He almost turned around and went back, but changed his mind when he remembered how itchy and smelly he was. It could wait until tomorrow morning."

"MAYOR ORDERS SWEEP OF DOWNTOWN STREETS . . . POLICE RAZE SKID ROW SHANTY TOWNS . . . HUNDREDS OF HOMELESS MOVED TO TEMPORARY SHELTERS."

Tannis saw the headlines on the front page of the *Los Padres Daily Bulletin* even before she sat down to breakfast. Her bowl of Shredded Wheat and her glass of orange juice landed fortuitously on the table as she snatched up the paper and sank with it into a chair.

"Oh, no," she whispered, turning cold. "They can't do this!" Quickly she lowered the newspaper and scanned the article, trying to assimilate it, but instead of the words she saw faces—frightened, bewildered faces.

Where would they go? What would they do? A cardboard box wasn't much, but it was better than nothing. This "sweep" wasn't offering any solutions—it was like sweeping dirt under a rug! And nobody seemed to care about what was going to happen to the people. People like Tannis's friend Binnie. What would become of her shopping cart if she were forced to go to a shelter? Binnie's cart was everything in the world to her; losing it would be like having her home burn to the ground. And poor Clarence, so claustrophobic he couldn't even go indoors long enough to use the rest room. He'd go crazy in a shelter, freak out completely, and those cops wouldn't understand. They'd just think he was a lunatic, and they'd try to restrain him, and that would make it worse.

"They can't do this," she said again, bringing her fist down on the newspaper with unfortunate consequences for the cereal bowl underneath. As the milk dripped off the table and puddled on the tile floor, Tannis was already in the garage, lifting her helmet off the handle-bars of her Honda.

"I don't know what to do," she said to Gunner a little while later. "This just makes me so *angry*."

"Anger's fine," Gunner drawled in the soft rumble that seemed to come from deep inside his massive chest. "Temper isn't." His eyes rested on her, serene and soothing as hot chocolate on a winter's day. Tannis looked down at the helmet in her hands and bit back a comment.

"You want to fight City Hall," Gunner went on in his unhurried way, "you got to fight their way, you follow me? Won't do you any good, now, to go chargin' up there throwin' temper tantrums."

There probably wasn't another person in the world, Tannis reflected, who could make her feel like a chastened child without also making her resent him for doing it. She was glad she'd stopped by the newsstand first; seeing Gunner always helped her get things in perspective.

The newsstand's counter, built to the specifications of Gunner's wheelchair, was a good height for sitting on. Tannis sat on it, balancing her helmet on her knee with one hand while she dragged her hair back from her face with the other. She filled her lungs, exhaled, wiggled her shoulders, and focused on the autographed photograph of Roy Campanella on the post behind Gunner's head. "Okay," she said, "I'm calm."

Gunner chuckled approvingly. "Atta, babe. Now, what you gotta understand about City Hall is, there's nobody up there but bureaucrats and politicians, and those kind of people don't understand emotions. You gotta talk to people in a language they *will* understand. Bureaucrats, now, all they understand is rules and forms. The only way to talk to a bureaucrat is to fill out a form. Politicians are a different breed of cat." He propped one elbow on the arm of his chair and leaned on it, unconsciously flexing his fingers while he stared at nothing, thinking.

Tannis waited quietly, watching massive muscles and ropelike tendons play beneath the mahogany skin of Gunner's arm. She figured if anybody knew how to deal with bureaucracy, it was Gunner. He'd lost his legs in the service of his country. In the years since, he'd probably been through more battles with paper-pushers and politicians than he'd ever had with the Viet Cong.

Gunner chuckled, breaking the silence. "I'll tell you how to get a politician's attention. You just talk 'image' to him—he'll listen. Don't waste your time tellin' him about right or wrong, about people gettin' hurt. Tell him how it's gonna hurt his image. You dig?"

Tannis nodded, grinning. "Yeah, I dig. Thanks, Gunner." She hopped off the counter and leaned over to kiss his cheek.

"Atta, babe," Gunner said softly. "Go get 'em, sugar."

City Hall was not a happy place this morning, Dillon observed as he heard the receptionist say for the fourth or fifth time, "I'm sorry, the mayor isn't in his office at the moment. Can someone else help you?"

Mayor Flintridge was famous for his folksy approach to city government. He was fond of expounding on the fact that while during his tenure as mayor Los Padres had grown from a small desert town to a not-so-small city, all the doors of City Hall, including his, remained open and accessible to all its citizens. Now, however, having chucked a rock into the hornet's nest, the mayor had apparently run for cover. Which was probably an astute move on his part, but one that had left the resulting furor in the hands of council members short-sighted enough to show up at City Hall today. So far, that included the office staff, Dillon, and Maude Harrington, the only woman on the council. Fred Gould and Don McNeil had businesses elsewhere to give them a reasonable excuse for absence; presumably, they'd show up in time for the emergency session Flintridge had called for two o'clock this afternoon. Meanwhile, Dillon, Maude, and the receptionist were coping as best they could.

"Councilman James?" Sally, the receptionist, was standing in the doorway.

"Dillon," he said, smiling at her. "Just Dillon."

"Okay . . . Dillon," Sally said, returning the smile. "I guess this one's yours. Mrs. Harrington is still talking to that guy from the L.A. *Times*. Can you take it?"

"Phone?"

"No, somebody to see the mayor. No appointment, but she said she'd speak to another council member, and I thought, if you were free . . ."

Something in the receptionist's voice pricked Dillon's curiosity. "Reporter?" he asked, frowning.

"I don't think so. I wouldn't bother you with it, except that . . . well, I just think you might want to talk to this one, sir."

"Well . . ." Dillon glanced at his watch. Not even ten o'clock. It was going to be a long day. "All right." He sighed. "I guess you might as well send her in."

In the fourth floor reception area Tannis was pacing. She was trying hard to hang on to the mood of confidence and control Gunner had restored in her, but it was a losing battle. If there was anything Tannis hated, it was being given the bureaucratic runaround.

"Ms. Winter? Right this way, please."

Tannis stared at the receptionist, a perfectly ordinary-looking woman with a pleasant face and dark hair, as if she'd arrived in a puff of smoke.

"Councilman James will be happy to answer your questions," the receptionist added, smiling.

Thinking, I'll just *bet* he will, Tannis tucked her helmet into the crook of her arm and followed the receptionist into a paneled hallway.

"First door on your right," the receptionist told her, then went back to the outer office.

The door was ajar. Tannis paused in front of it, frowning. There wasn't any name on the panel, nor any sound from within. She was lifting her hand to knock when a dry but not unpleasant voice said, "You're in the right place—they just haven't gotten around to painting my name on the door yet. Please, come in."

Tannis took a deep breath, set her jaw, and entered the room with a firm and purposeful step. Momentum carried her halfway to the desk before an uncomfortable pressure in her chest reminded her to exhale. She halted. For one of the few times in her life, she was at a loss for words.

Councilman Dillon James sure wasn't what she'd expected.

Three

He was waiting for her, politely standing behind his desk, wearing a conservative gray suit and dark tie. His hair was dark brown, wavy, and, surprisingly, a little too long. And though that seemed at odds with the way he was dressed, in some inexplicable way Tannis felt that it suited him.

He was very tall and rather too thin, she thought. His stance seemed relaxed and careless, but there was nothing lackadaisical about him. His glance was interested, alert, and his movements, as he leaned across the desk to briefly clasp her hand, had an economical grace that suggested he was also very fit.

Like his body, his face was long, angular, and undeniably attractive. His nose was aquiline, his chin just short of pugnacious, his eyes set deep and shadowed by thick, dark lashes. Two sets of grooves etched his cheeks, the inner set bracketing his smile like parentheses, the outer ones smaller, almost dimples. He looked familiar to her. She kept trying to think whom he reminded her of—some movie actor, she supposed; she was never very good at recalling things like that.

One thing she did know. All in all, Councilman James was the most interesting looking man she'd met in a long time. She decided she might have to rethink her long-standing prejudice against politicians.

Belatedly realizing, as she took the seat he indicated, that he had said something, Tannis cleared her throat and blurted out, "I beg your pardon?"

A gleam of amusement twinkled through his thicket of lashes. "I said, please call me Dillon. How can I help you, Ms. . . . ?"

"Uh . . ." Tannis said, and only just managed to add, "Winter." Her throat had suddenly gone so dry, all she could do was whisper.

She didn't understand it. The way she was feeling reminded her of her very first foray into show business. On that memorable occasion, when she was about nine, she'd been chosen for the honor of reciting "Twas the Night Before Christmas" for the school Christmas program. She had stepped confidently into the spotlight, looked out upon the vast sea of faces—and developed total though temporary paralysis.

"Ms. Winter?" the councilman prompted kindly, and waited.

Tannis abruptly leaned over to place her helmet on the floor, a movement which seemed to help restore the flow of blood to her brain. This is ridiculous, she thought. How could she possibly have stage fright? This man was nothing but a lousy politician! *Gunner*, she thought, searching through her memory for his calm, intelligent eyes, *Help!*

Straightening up with her wits more or less intact, she fixed the politician with a forthright glare and murmured, "I'm sorry. I guess I'm just a little upset right now."

The councilman's eyebrows went up, and Tannis thought the look in his eyes had grown a bit wary. *He thinks I'm a nut case.* She took a deep, fortifying breath.

"It's okay," she assured him with a wry smile. "I'm not going to freak out or anything."

The councilman looked amused. "Oh, good."

"I just think when it comes to feelings, it's best not to equivocate. Mr. James—"

"Dillon," the councilman interrupted smoothly. "Just call me Dillon. Ms. Winter, I'm sorry you're upset. Maybe if you told me what you're upset about, I might be able to help you." He sounded very patient. Tannis almost laughed, recognizing the same tone, and almost the same words, she might have used to interview a patient in danger of becoming irrational.

"Actually," she said, "I had hoped to speak with Mayor Flintridge . . ."

Suddenly she felt frustrated and unfocused, as if she'd somehow lost her way. The problem was, she'd come loaded for a politician, and the bull's-eye in her mind wore George Flintridge's face. With his jowly mug and florid style, the mayor was the epitome of the small-town politician. All the things she and Gunner had talked about, all the speeches she'd rehearsed on the way over here, had been aimed directly at Mayor Flintridge. Presented instead with this tall, rock-jawed, soft-spoken man, Tannis felt disoriented; she knew her lines all right, but somehow she had the feeling she was in the wrong play.

"Do you know what's going on?" she asked finally, her habitual bluntness coming to her rescue.

The councilman looked blank for a moment, and then that smile lighted his face. "Well, most of the time I do, although it has been only two weeks since I was sworn in. I imagine I have quite a bit of catching up to do." Amusement made a pleasant ripple in his voice. "What is it you're referring to?"

"*That.*" Tannis reached across the desk to stab the newspaper that was pinioned to his blotter by one of his elbows. "This . . . this police sweep. These Gestapo tactics. This—"

"Come now, Ms. Winter. Hardly the Gestapo." He still spoke with patience, and even a touch of amusement, but his jaw had a new solidity, his eyes a new kind of glitter that though she knew she couldn't have encountered it before, somehow stirred her memory like a breath of air on a windless day. *Who did he remind her of?*

She snorted. "Not far from it!" Too agitated to stay anchored to a chair, she jumped up and paced to the window, rubbing her arms, surprised to discover goose bumps there. She heard the scrape of Dillon's chair. "Do you know," she said, tapping the window glass, trying to ignore the nervous tremors in the back of her neck that told her he was coming near, "that right down there on those streets there are people being deprived of their rights and their possessions just on the whim of some politicians?"

She whirled, ready to fix the councilman with her best glare and continue her impassioned appeal. In the next moment, however, her words expired with her breath, feeble and unspoken. A few feet away from her Dillon James had come to a halt as if the words she'd hurled at him had been bricks forming a solid wall in his path. The expression on his face seemed stunned, as if he'd run headlong into it.

Good heavens, she wondered, what did I say? She wondered if maybe she'd insulted him, saying all those things about politicians. Her and her big mouth! She hoped she hadn't made him angry. Quite suddenly she knew that the last thing she wanted was to have this man angry with her.

And yet, he didn't look like an angry man, or one with wounded feelings. Smiling again, he joined her at the window, but now there was something different about his smile. As he looked down at her, the harsh light unveiled his eyes, and in their depths Tannis saw a gleam of appraisal. Once again that elusive memory wafted through her mind, bringing with it a faint but tantalizing whiff of déjà vu.

"Ms. Winter," Dillon drawled, thoughtfully rubbing

the side of his jaw, "would you mind telling me just what your interest is in all of this?" The question was polite, and asked with a smile. Even so, there was something about it that suggested Dillon James was a man accustomed to having his questions answered promptly—and truthfully.

"I'm a social psychologist," Tannis replied, relieved that his cautiousness had so simple an explanation. "I'm sorry—I didn't realize I hadn't explained."

"Ah," Dillon said, nodding. "A psychologist. Should I be calling you *Doctor* Winter?"

"Well, no." she smiled. "Not yet, but I'm working on it. And you can call me Tannis. I'm here because as my research project for my doctorate in sociology I've been studying the problems of the homeless—more specifically, the inveterate homeless. The ones for whom the street life is so deeply ingrained they don't know how to live any other way. The ones who, given any choice at all, will go right on living on the streets no matter what you do to try to help them. Mr. James, those people—"

"Dillon."

"Dillon. Those people don't want to go to a shelter. They're suspicious of the shelters, even afraid, some of them. It's the same as jail to them, don't you see? And forcing them into shelters is like putting them in jail without due process."

He looked at her thoughtfully and released a long breath as he said, "I see. . . ."

Elation poured through her. "Then you'll help? You'll put a stop to it?"

"What?" He blinked and seemed surprised, as if his mind had just come back from somewhere else. "I'm sorry." His smile was gentle again. "There's not much I can do."

"But why? Surely the council—"

"It wasn't a council decision. Mayor Flintridge ordered the cleanup himself."

"Can he do that?" Tannis asked, dismayed.

Dillon chuckled. "Oh, yes, certainly."

"But *why*? Why now, all of a sudden? Usually nobody pays any attention to the street people except to give them a wide berth when they pass them on the sidewalk!"

"You sound as if you know what it's like," Dillon said softly, touching her arm. The contact his hand made with her skin produced a tiny frisson, the smallest of shocks.

Her breath caught. "I do," she said.

"Well." Dillon cleared his throat and pulled his hand away from her, rubbing his fingers against his palm as if it itched. "I believe," he said, frowning, "that the, ah, current situation was prompted by a recent incident that was, through an unfortunate set of circumstances, brought to the mayor's attention."

"An incident?" Tannis asked. Dillon nodded. He had that curious air of watchfulness again, almost of expectancy. Tannis was beginning to think it was just a quirk of his nature.

"Yeah," he went on, his tone one of dark amusement, "it seems there was an altercation downtown yesterday morning between two, uh, denizens of the streets. During said altercation, which was witnessed, in part, by two of Los Padres's finest, a bag lady apparently struck a"—Dillon coughed—"a gentleman—"

"Ha!"

"I beg your pardon?"

"Nothing," Tannis said hastily, trying to look innocent. "Go on."

"Yes . . . well." He gave her an intent look and went on in a carefully neutral voice. "Apparently the aforementioned bag lady struck said *gentleman* with her shopping cart in an anatomical region commonly referred to as 'below the belt.' "

"Well," Tannis mumbled, feeling guilty. "I'm sure he had it coming to him."

Dillon growled. Before his lashes dropped to veil his eyes, Tannis caught an odd gleam in them. After a moment he cleared his throat and went on. "In any case, said gentleman was left sitting in the gutter in an, uh, incapacitated state, where he attracted the attention of the aforementioned police officers, who mistook his condition for inebriation—I beg your pardon, did you say something?"

"No," replied Tannis, unsuccessfully smothering a spurt of mirth. "Please, go on."

After giving her a quelling glance, he continued somewhat sardonically. "Subsequently, as I said, the affair came to the attention of the mayor, who for some reason didn't think that quarreling indigents were good for Los Padres's public image. Just doesn't appeal to snowbound easterners trying to decide where to spend their winter vacation dollars."

Tannis was gazing at him in disbelief. "So," she said slowly, "Gunner was right—it's just a matter of image after all."

"Gunner?" Dillon said, looking perplexed. "Who's Gunner?"

She sighed and turned back to the window. "He's a friend of mine. You ought to talk to him sometime. He runs the newsstand down on Fifth and Cleveland. He runs it from a wheelchair because he lost his legs in Vietnam. He got his name there too—Gunner. He was the trigger man on one of those helicopter gun ships. He lived on the streets for a while when he was out of a job and couldn't afford the rent for the kind of place that would accommodate his wheelchair. Now he's got a ground floor apartment way over on South Palm. He commutes—by wheelchair. He doesn't mind that, though, because it helps him keep in shape. Gunner's a wheelchair athlete—plays wheelchair basketball and runs wheelchair marathons. Things like that."

"Sounds like quite a guy."

Dillon's voice was soft, slightly raspy, and very near.

She could feel him there, close behind her, and deep down inside her she felt the faint, tight tremblings of sexual awareness. She glanced nervously at him, and then quickly back toward the window, afraid her response to him might be visible somehow.

"Do you remember that really cold winter we had, oh, maybe two or three years ago?" When he nodded, she reached out to spread her hand against the cool glass and leaned forward so she could see the street and the park below. "It got so cold that year that a couple of street people actually died of hypothermia, so the city decided to move them indoors. Which was *fine*, a really decent, humanitarian thing to do, right?" She turned to face Dillon, her eyes shining with emotion. "Yeah, right—and for most people it was. But the . . . people in charge were so eager to get everybody off the streets, they forgot they were dealing with people, not animals. They just herded the masses indoors without taking into consideration the particular needs of each individual. They put Gunner in a third floor room in one of those downtown firetrap hotels—you know the ones? The elevators were broken. Do you know what that means to someone like Gunner? He couldn't even make it to the rescue missions to get food!"

She felt Dillon's hands on her arms, just below the shoulders. "Hey," he said softly, "I'm sorry. But those things happen when you're trying to deal with a lot of people in a complicated situation."

Tannis stood very still, looking away from him, fighting for control. His nearness was upsetting, but she didn't want to move away from him. "Yes," she said huskily after a while, "but that's the point. It *is* complicated, and they *are* people—not faceless entities called 'the homeless.' Someone needs to know who they are, and what their individual needs are. I could tell you so many stories. . . . There's Binnie, who used to have her own home until her husband died and left her penniless. Her shopping cart is all she's got, and it's precious—"

"Tannis . . ." His hands slipped down her arms, and his thumbs began stroking the soft skin at the inner bend of her elbows.

She shivered and pulled away from him, regretting her action a moment later when the warmth of his touch faded. "Nobody cares about those people!" she cried, more angry with herself and her runaway responses than with Dillon, or even the mayor. "What you're doing now isn't a solution, it's just a . . . a salve for somebody's pride!"

"Listen, I assure you, we *are* concerned about the people living out there. *I'm* concerned."

"Bull pucky!" Tannis shouted, flinging an arm out and whacking her hand against the windowpane with a force she felt to her shoulder. "If you were really concerned, you'd be down there in the streets, where you could see what's going on, instead of sitting up here in your cozy little office with your nice, pretty bird's-eye view of the world! If you really care, why don't you get out there yourself and see what it's like!"

There was a long silence, during which Tannis suddenly remembered that she was yelling at a city councilman. The fires of her anger died and became the cold, dismal sludge of embarrassment. She was opening her mouth to begin an apology, when she noticed that the city councilman was smiling. True, it was a funny little half smile, but a smile nonetheless.

"That sounds a lot like a challenge," he said softly.

So instead of apologizing for her outburst, Tannis brought her chin up, looked him straight in the eye, and said, "I guess it does."

"Well?"

"Well, what?" Her heart was suddenly beating hard and fast, as if she'd been running.

"Are you issuing me a challenge?" His gaze moved over her face and came to rest on her lips.

For some reason her lips grew warm and began to tingle. Unable to help herself, she licked them. "Yes," she said huskily, "I guess I am."

His chuckle had a different timbre, one she felt in her body's depths rather than heard. "I always enjoy a challenge." The dimplelike creases appeared briefly, then vanished. "Shall we?"

"Shall we what?" Tannis whispered, feeling confused.

"Shake on it."

She felt something touch her arm. Tearing her fascinated gaze from his face, she looked down and found his hand waiting. "Oh," she said on a breath, and placed hers into it, palm against palm. It was warm and dry and smooth—a nice enough hand. There was no reason why tiny electric shocks should originate from that contact and go racing up her arm, making her feel weak and nerveless.

"Challenge accepted," Dillon said. His expression was grave, but behind the veil of lashes Tannis caught a gleam that made her wonder whether he was responding to another, unspoken challenge.

Excitement stirred through her like a breeze through wind chimes, making all her senses sing. Holding back an unanticipated bubble of laughter, she moved her fingers within his grasp, rubbing them over the back of his hand. The contact altered subtly, becoming not so much a clasp as a holding.

"So," Dillon said softly, "where do we go from here?"

And this time, with instincts she hadn't even realized she possessed, Tannis knew the question had a dual purpose. *Where do we go from here? What's in store for us?*

All at once excitement became panic. *Too close!* something in her protested. *Too soon!* Pulling her hand from his, she began to speak rapidly, and with nervous gestures.

"Well, you just have to get out there, into the street, the sooner the better. I can go with you . . . introduce you to people." She paused, not sure whether that was too pushy or not. "At least at first," she went on hurriedly. "I know the places where they hide—"A thought struck her. "Look, I *can* trust you, can't I? You're not using me just to get to them? Because if you are—"

"You can trust me. My word of honor. Listen—" He glanced at the watch on his wrist. "It's almost eleven. Why don't you meet me across the street in the park at . . . shall we say, noon? That'll give me time to take care of some things I need to do. We can have lunch and talk details. How's that?" His eyes held hers, the light in them as brilliant as sunlight on water.

Tannis hesitated, chewing on her lower lip. Could she trust him? A moment ago she'd have bet her life on it. Now she wasn't so sure. If only she could be certain he was sincere in his desire to know and understand the problems street people had to face every day. . . .

An idea began to form in her mind, a way of testing Councilman James's attitude and intentions. The more she thought about it, the better she liked it. The only thing she wondered was whether she'd have time to go home and change her clothes. There was plenty of time to get home on her scooter, but probably not enough to make it back to City Center Park on foot. Maybe if she left the shopping cart behind and came on the scooter . . .

Yes! she thought, feeling a surge of excitement. It would work. If she met Councilman James as Win the bag lady, she would be able to test his attitudes and possibly even give him a graphic illustration of her point. She'd do it!

"All right," she said equably, carefully masking her inner feelings. "Sounds great. Meet you in front of the statue of Father Serra in an hour."

"I'm looking forward to it," Dillon said softly.

Tannis paused in the doorway to glance back at him. Her heart paused, too, and then went on in a new, bumpier rhythm. "So am I," she said. "See you."

After she'd gone, Dillon stayed where he was with one arm propped against the wall by the window, gazing thoughtfully down on the street below. It occurred to him that he was waiting for something, and when he saw a tiny foreshortened figure wearing a yellow sweater and a shiny black helmet cross the street to the parking meters adjacent to the park, he knew what that something was.

Not even aware that he was grinning, he watched her straddle a yellow scooter, pause to fasten the helmet's chin strap, then pull carefully out of a parking space. A moment later the scooter and its rider were arrowing down the street, disturbing the morning's serenity like an angry bumblebee.

So *that's* my bag lady! Dillon thought. His laughter rang out loud in the room, bringing the receptionist to his door. Still chortling, he apologized and sent her away, shaking her head and wondering.

Some bag lady, he thought; not quite what he'd expected. *Suspect: Female Caucasian; age, approximately thirty; height, five feet six . . . maybe seven; weight, a hundred twenty pounds, nicely arranged; hair, honey-brown, straight, worn long but with a layered cut . . . warm, windblown . . . like sun-ripened wheat; eyes, winter gray, ice-blue, fire and ice.*

Hold it! What the hell kind of police report was this anyway?

Distinguishing marks: freckles, irregular upper lip, small chip on shoulder.

Thoughtfully now, Dillon rubbed at his jaw. That was a problem. The woman was certainly sincere, and some of her sentiments weren't all that different from his own, but she had a lot to learn about life on the streets. Shoot, her concept of the kind of people who lived out there sounded like something right out of *Cannery Row!* She'd been lucky so far, but sooner or later she was going to find out that this wasn't Steinbeck country. The wolves were out there, and she was just a lamb in sheep's clothing. She was going to get hurt unless she developed some better instincts for self-preservation.

Dillon looked at his watch and frowned. What that woman needed was a little taste of reality, and maybe, just maybe, he knew a way to give it to her. He'd give her a scare—just a little one. It was for her own good. And besides, he told himself with a certain visceral anticipation, he owed her one for that number she'd done on him yesterday.

Crossing with long strides to his desk, he reached for his phone and punched a button. When Sally answered, he asked for the chief of police.

After a surprisingly short wait he heard Logan's voice.

"Buddy," Dillon said, "I need a favor."

"After yesterday, I don't owe you any favors."

"Put it on my tab. Listen, I'm going back on the street for a little while this afternoon. Under the circumstances, I don't think it would be a good idea if the sort of misunderstanding that occurred yesterday were to repeat itself—if you get my meaning?"

"Dillon," Logan said with a sigh, "you're nuts."

"I know. So listen—put the word out, okay? I'll be the one in the Dodger cap and the crummy brown jacket. You remember the wardrobe? Oh, and Logan? Tell the boys to cut me a little slack, okay?"

"Dillon, what the hell are you asking of me?"

"Trust me," Dillon said, and hung up. He just barely had time to get home and change.

As he stared out of the office, he suddenly stopped and ran a hand over his jaw. What he felt gave him a moment's pause, but there wasn't much he could do about it. Tannis hadn't recognized him so far, he was sure of that; but he wasn't at all sure how far he was going to get with this little game plan of his without a weekend's growth of stubble.

· · ·

The woman who slipped her scooter into a parking space near City Center Park at five minutes before noon wore a faded, shapeless dress, three pairs of mismatched socks, and a pair of man's shoes several sizes too big for her. Over the dress, in spite of the balmy temperatures, she wore a sweater in a bilious shade of green, and a too-large, once-stylish coat. Wisps of thin gray hair that had managed to escape the confines of a purple knit cap hung lank on her neck and forehead. The hands that nervously clutched a large, shabby shoulder bag were encased in brown wool gloves. She'd gotten a few funny looks, driving a yellow Honda through the streets and boulevards of Los Padres like that, but Tannis didn't care. She was filled with excitement, anticipation, a strange, effervescent joy.

All of which had nothing to do with having met Councilman Dillon James, she told herself. Or if it did, it was because he'd listened to her, because she'd actually gotten through to him, and because someone was finally going to do something about solving the *real* problems of the homeless! It had nothing whatsoever to do with his enigmatic eyes, or the smile that seemed to burst across his austere face like a sunrise, or the tingling sensation she felt on her skin wherever he touched her.

No, she insisted, she was happy because she just had a feeling that this meeting with Dillon was going to make wonderful things happen. And besides, it was such a beautiful day!

I must be a winter's child, she thought as she settled herself at the base of the statue of Father Junipero Serra, the founder of California's Spanish missions. She'd always loved winter, the California kind, anyway, which was the only kind she'd ever known. She loved the anomalies, contradictions, the infinite variety of California winters. She loved experiencing the full spectrum of seasons, sometimes in the space of a few days. She loved the fact that she could drive to the mountains and find snow and go skiing even on warm days like this one; she loved cold clear nights and radiant days. She loved the parks, where the grass smelled young and fresh, where flowers bloomed in beds beneath the winter-bare branches of deciduous trees.

I love this, she thought. Sitting in the sun at high noon with a soft breeze blowing, feeling neither too hot nor too cold, waiting for something exciting to happen . . .

A hand touched her arm, then encircled it with a firm masculine grip. In that instant, as her heart cried *Dillon!* in joyful recognition, Tannis knew for the first time that her heart really was a mechanism—a pump, a faulty one, obviously in dire need of repair. It seemed to operate in surges and falters, sending too much blood here and not enough there.

"Dillon," she said faintly, turning toward him.

She felt her heart conk out completely; she felt herself go bloodless and cold. It wasn't Dillon's face that looked down into hers, but the dark, dangerous face of the derelict.

Four

The wino in the baseball cap towered over her, reeking
of sweat and alcohol. He was swaying and coughing
and holding a handkerchief to his mouth as if he'd just
been, or was about to be violently sick.

Adrenaline assumed command of Tannis' functions,
kicking her heart into a smooth, accelerating rhythm.
"Please," she cried, wrenching her arm from his grasp.
"Leave me alone!"

The derelict attempted to recapture her arm, and
instead managed to clutch the shoulder of her coat.

"What do you want?" she gasped in a high, ineffec-
tual voice, shrinking into the collar of her coat like a
turtle trying to disappear inside its shell.

"Hey," the wino wheezed, "I jess wanna know why
you hadda go an *hit* me. You didn't haf t'do that. You
know, you hit me right in the—"

Holding herself rigid, Tannis said staunchly, "Let go
of me, or I'm going to start screaming."

"An' that *hurts!*" the man finished indignantly, ignoring the threat.

"I'm surprised you could feel anything," Tannis muttered, and was instantly sorry. The man obviously wasn't
as far gone as she'd thought, not too far gone to take

offense anyway. Above the handkerchief his eyes took on an ominous gleam. Strong fingers crawled over her shoulder and fastened on her collar.

Until that moment Tannis had been more startled and dismayed by the unexpected reappearance of the wino than anything. But now fear gripped her, seizing her suddenly, as it had the day before. Still trying to disappear inside the coat, she darted a quick look around, searching desperately for some source of help. Where in the world was Dillon? Where was anyone? It was high noon! This was City Center Park! Where was everybody?

The answer was clear. Everyone—the shoppers, the city employees and downtown office workers on lunch break, all the well-dressed, well-fed people—were giving them a wide berth, not at all eager, it seemed, to involve themselves in a sordid and unpleasant scene between a couple of skid-row derelicts.

But the police! Where in the world were the police, she wondered. Weren't they supposed to be in the middle of a big "sweep of downtown streets?" Why weren't they sweeping right here, and now! Why was it there was never a cop around when you needed one?

Where was Dillon?

It came to her then like the calm that follows a clap of thunder: no one was going to help her. She was on her own.

She stood very still for a moment, listening to the quiet voice of reality. And then, without giving herself a chance to think about it, she hauled off and kicked the wino in the shins.

"Ow! *Shoot!*"

But the man didn't quite relinquish his grip on her collar. So while he was hopping on one foot and rubbing his shin, Tannis simply wriggled out of her coat and left him holding nothing but cloth. As she darted away across the grass, she could hear him swearing.

And then she heard another sound, one that gave

her a new infusion of adrenaline. Running footsteps, pounding hard. Without looking back she stepped out of her shoes and ran for her life.

"Tannis! Wait!"

She heard, but it didn't register; panic was governing her mind. The derelict was right behind her, gaining on her! She could hear him breathing, feel the heat of his body.

When she felt hard hands grip her arms from behind, she fought with the strength that comes from sheer terror. But the wino was stronger—and soberer—than he looked. In a matter of seconds he had her arms pinned to her sides and her body locked tight against his. She felt heated muscle, quivering sinew, and the thump of a hard-working heart against her back. A bony chin bit hard on her temple. Knowing it was pointless to fight anymore, Tannis pressed her lips together, shut her eyes tightly, and listened to the sobbing sounds of her own breathing and the heavy rasp of his.

"Okay," a soft, out-of-breath voice said, "that's better."

It was a moment or two before Tannis realized it wasn't the wino's voice she was hearing. Her body stiffened.

"Tannis?" Sensing her stillness, he went on cautiously. "I'm going to let go of you now . . . okay?"

A warm breath smelling of nothing more offensive than cinnamon gum sighed past her ear. His rigid muscles relaxed. His hands, gentle now, gripped her arms and slowly turned her.

"Tannis? Hey, are you okay now?" The voice sounded rusty and concerned.

Tannis found herself staring fixedly at a dirty gray sweatshirt and a chest that was still moving rapidly in and out. Strong fingers touched her chin and pulled it up, and she looked into thick-lashed eyes shaded by the visor of a baseball cap and narrowed to a frown.

Now one had ever accused Tannis of having an even

disposition. She had a temper, as all of her family and friends knew very well, the kind that ignites in an instant, burns quick and hot, and as quickly shimmers into nothing, like fireworks in a summer sky. Her loved ones were used to it, and so was she. But at that moment her fury was so real, she'd have sworn that she'd never known even a hint of anger before.

"You . . . *bastard!*" she hissed. And then, somehow, she managed to grip the shoulder bag in her hand. With all her might she swung it, and heard a most satisfying "Whap!" as it connected with the side of Councilman Dillon James's head.

Without so much as a glance or a pause to assess the damage, she whirled and stalked away. She moved as rapidly as she dared under the circumstances, trusting providence to keep her from disaster, because, as always, the firestorm had passed quickly and, as always, in its aftermath came the tears.

For the second time in a very few minutes Dillon said, "Ow!" And then, with a great deal of feeling, *"Damn!"* He reflected ruefully as he nursed the tender place on his head. That he must have done more swearing in the last five minutes alone than in all the years since leaving the department.

Well, he thought philosophically as he bent over to pick up his baseball cap, he'd gotten what he deserved for becoming involved with a beautiful woman crazy enough to go around dressed up like a bag lady.

Feeling a trickle on his forehead, he made a ginger exploration with his fingers and discovered a sticky warmth. The clasp on that purse of hers, he thought; it must have cut him. One heck of a weapon, that was. One heck of a lady too—good at picking unusual weapons. First a shopping cart, and now this. He'd been a pretty tough cop in his day, but so far he was oh-for-two with this babe.

As he stood watching the lady in question go stalking off across the lawn, Dillon's feelings were definitely mixed. On the one hand, he hadn't suffered this much damage to his physical person since the last time he'd tried to break up a fight between a hooker and her pimp. He wasn't a masochist; his self-preservation instincts were hollering at him to let her go, leave her alone, stay away from her.

On the other hand, he'd asked for it. And once he got past the pain, he had to admit it was pretty funny: two grown people trying to outguess each other, both dressing up in disguises to try to teach the other a lesson. She was funny, in that purple cap, that godawful dress and sweater, stomping across the park in her stocking feet. She was funny, and after this morning's brief glimpse he knew beyond any doubt that underneath all those shapeless clothes she had a very nice body indeed—lean, but soft enough to feel good in his arms.

But on the other hand, he'd never seen such a temper! Why would he want to mess around with something that volatile? Life was hazardous enough as it was.

But on the other hand . . . The way she looked right then, walking away from him, reminded Dillon of something. The hunched shoulders, the stiff-necked, jerky-legged walk . . . It was the attitude he'd had as a kid, pride-wounded and chastised, trying so darn hard not to cry.

Dillon, he said to himself with a sigh as he went jogging after her, you're as nutty as she is.

"Tannis," he panted, catching up with her, "wait. Please." She slowed and stopped. He wasn't sure what he expected her to do, but when he saw her pull a hand surreptitiously across her eyes before she turned, something odd happened to his insides. He had an impulse to put his arms around her, to pull her close and comfort her. But because he understood her pride, he only touched her arm and said softly, "Hey, listen, I'm sorry." He was amazed at how sorry he was—not that he'd scared her, because that had been his intention, but because he seemed to have wounded her in some way he didn't understand.

"You're . . . *sorry?*" she said in a blurred voice, lifting her face sideways to look at him. "Why did you do that to me?"

Dillon shrugged and muttered, "To scare you, as a matter of fact."

"To scare me? Why? Because of . . . what I did to you yesterday?"

"No!" Dillon felt a sense of shock and a twinge of guilt for that modicum of revenge that had been in his heart. "Lord, no. What do you think I am? I did it to make a point! It *is* dangerous on the streets, Tannis, and I don't think you realize that."

She sniffed. "You knew who I was, didn't you? When I came to your office this morning. You knew I was the bag lady who—"

"No, I didn't," Dillon said. "Not at first."

"Why didn't you say anything? Why did you let me think you hadn't recognized me?"

Dillon frowned. "I'm not sure. I wasn't sure at first whether or not you recognized *me*. You told me you were studying the problems of the homeless, so the fact that you'd dressed like one of them in order to do that made sense. After all, I'd just been doing the same thing, and I hadn't wanted the world to know about it either. What I don't understand is why you did *this*. I've got to tell you, it came as quite a surprise."

"*You* were surprised!" She gave a watery gurgle of laughter and then was silent, her head slightly cocked, as if she were listening to something. "I wanted . . ." She turned abruptly. He heard a sniff and saw her swipe again at her eyes. Under the awful green sweater her shoulders lifted, then settled. "You said things this morning, but talking's so easy. I wanted to find out what your real feelings were—deep down, gut-level feelings. People react instinctively to those who are different from themselves. I wanted to see how you responded to me . . . as a bag lady. I didn't know—"

"A test of my character?" Dillon said dryly. He touched her shoulder and added softly, "I responded to you yesterday, or had you forgotten? I gave you a flower."

"Yes, but I didn't know that was you."

Her voice was drowned and defenseless; amazing, the effect it had on him. He found that although he was staring at the pompon on her cap and at the strings of gray hair sneaking into the collar of her drab dress, he was seeing her instead as she'd looked in his office that morning: A slender young woman with summer sunshine in her hair and skin, and winter fires in her eyes. . . .

"Instead, I found out . . ." Her voice trembled and died.

"I hurt you," Dillon said, running his fingers back and forth across the top of her shoulder. "I didn't mean to do that. I'm sorry."

"No!" she denied, shaking her head. "I suppose it's ironic, really. Here I was trying to test your character, and I failed my own test. I thought I was so tolerant, so understanding, so *aware*. And I reacted to you with the same blind fear and prejudice—" She pressed the heels of her hands angrily against her eyes. "Oh, damn."

It was strange, Dillon thought. Seeing her so hurt and whipped only made him remember more vividly the way she'd sailed into his office that morning—vibrant and bursting with self-confidence. He'd wanted to give her a little dose of reality, yes, but he hadn't meant to destroy those things he'd admired so much in her. He suddenly realized he wanted that confidence and enthusiasm back. More than wanting, he *needed* it. He felt an infusion of energy and excitement inside himself. Like a light coming on in his head, he knew he needed this woman's passion, courage, and dedication working with him and for him on this homeless problem.

He put both hands on her shoulders and squeezed gently. Her body felt tense, rigid, and incredibly vulnerable. "Are you this hard on everybody, or just yourself?"

She shuddered suddenly and turned to him, ignoring the tears she'd been trying so hard to hide. "Dillon, there's no getting around the fact that I reacted with fear, loathing, hostility, prejudice—all the emotions I've accused others of! I've been—oh . . . !"

Her eyes widened, and her mouth formed a blurred *O* of dismay. She squeaked, "Oh, God—" and reached impulsively to touch his temple. The glove on her hand made her pause. She gave it a look of revulsion, then snatched it off, and Dillon felt her fingers like the soft cool kiss of silk on his forehead. "I *hurt* you."

"Yeah, you were trying to, as I recall," he said, smiling. "Look, stop beating yourself to death with your own liberalism. Personally I think you acted with common sense and good judgment—not to mention ingenuity." He brushed away a moist streak on her cheek with the backs of his fingers, then drew his thumb across the bridge of her nose to intercept a fresh tear on the other side. "I'd have been a lot more worried about you if you hadn't—oh, my God!" For a heartbeat or two all he could do was stare in horror at the piece of her face that had come off in his fingers.

Tannis clapped a hand to her nose. She looked from his face to the scrap of flesh-colored latex dangling from his fingers, and then her composure simply erupted. With laughter bubbling up in her and flowing out of her like a kettle boiling over, she collapsed, howling, onto Dillon's chest.

Though her laughter was effervescent and joyous and he loved the sound of it, Dillon was too preoccupied to join in. For the time being, all he could do was stand there, gazing helplessly down at the purple pompon quivering just under his nose. The disparity between what she looked like at the moment and what he knew her to be was beginning to get to him.

He didn't seem to know what to do with his hands. They were flat against her shoulder blades, not quite holding her but not fending her off either. He found it an awkward and ambiguous position, one he wasn't accustomed to being in. Under the right circumstances, he wasn't a man to deny an impulse as strong as the one he was experiencing now, which was to wrap his arms around this woman and see if that felt as good as he thought it might. But to add to his inner confusion, it had come belatedly to his notice that the two of them were attracting a good deal of attention from the lunch crowd in the park.

A drunken brawl between two derelicts, it seemed, was a spectacle from which decent people gladly averted their eyes. A tender embrace between two derelicts was something else entirely.

"Uh, Tannis," Dillon said, uneasily patting her back, "don't you think this looks a little odd?"

She drew back, wiping her eyes, then sniffed and looked around dazedly. "Oh."

"Here—you'd better put this back on." He held up the piece of latex with a thumb and forefinger, controlling laughter only by keeping his voice stern and his features forbidding. "Let's get out of this circus before we become the main attraction. Is there someplace we can go?"

"I thought we were going to have lunch. I'm starving."

"I brought lunch. At least, I had it with me when I arrived. I'm not sure what I did with it when you, uh . . ."

"You brought lunch?"

"Well, yeah. I figured we couldn't go to a decent restaurant with me looking like this. Of course, I didn't realize at the time we were going to be a matched set. I stopped by a deli and picked up a couple of subs. I hope that's all right."

Tannis sighed and murmured, "Sounds wonderful." And she smiled that radiant, sunshine smile.

Dillon felt a familiar burst of warmth in his belly. He coughed and mumbled, "I think I probably dropped the sack back there with your coat. . . ."

As he went jogging off to retrieve it, he was thinking incredulously, I'm losing my mind. She looks like a molting pigeon. Can I possibly desire her?

Amazingly the bag of submarine sandwiches and potato salad was still on the grass where he'd dropped it, with Tannis's coat on top of it. He was inspecting the condition of the sandwiches, when she came up, shuffling again, since she'd stopped on the way to get her shoes.

"How are they?" She was looking at the sandwiches with undisguised hunger.

"Bruised but edible," Dillon pronounced, grimacing as he looked around. "Do you know someplace where we can go? Someplace a little less public?"

"I know a nice park bench." Tannis paused in the process of enveloping herself once more in her coat to give him an impish grin. "Nobody will pay any attention to us—bums are *supposed* to sit around on park benches."

As she listened to Dillon's chuckle of appreciation and watched the familiar grooves bracket his smile, Tannis felt a small explosion inside her, which wasn't unusual since she experienced life as a series of explosions—explosions of anger, enthusiasm, grief, joy, love. But this one was different, something she'd never felt before—a sweet, gentle awakening, like a flower's opening captured by the miracle of time-lapse photography.

How did I miss it, she wondered, stealing glances at him as they walked. How could I not have known who he was?

She should have recognized him the moment she'd walked into his office. He had such strong, distinctive features—those eyes, that hooked nose and angular chin!—and he hadn't done anything to alter them, as she had her own with cheek pads and latex. He'd fooled her with nothing but a baseball cap, a quarter-inch of stubble, a handkerchief, and some old clothes, while she, with all her makeup skills, hadn't fooled him for a minute.

"What?" he asked, catching her looking at him.

She shook her head. "Nothing." His eyes rested on her for a few moments while his smile slipped awry. She had to avert her eyes as warmth flooded her cheeks.

It was more than clothing and a little growth of beard, she decided. It was a whole attitude, a way of moving, standing, speaking; facial expressions, a certain look in the eyes. He'd cultivated a different personality, so completely different it even altered his physical appearance. And yet, he wore both identities so comfortably; each one had seemed absolutely believable and real.

As if, she thought, they were both a part of him—two sides of the same coin. The light and dark sides of Dillon James . . .

"Here's one," Tannis said as she picked out a bench in the warm sunshine overlooking a bed of pansies. As she sat, she peeled back her coat, then took off her gloves and stuffed them into one of her pockets.

"Why do you wear those?" Dillon asked, sitting beside her. "I've wondered."

Without a word Tannis held out her hands. Smooth, slender, young hands.

Dillon nodded. "Ah, I see. Dead giveaways." He held out one of the subs.

"Mmf," Tannis said, holding up a hand. "Wait a minute."

"So that's how you do that." Dillon watched with narrow-eyed interest as she removed the padding from inside her cheeks. "Amazing what a difference it makes."

"Not enough of a difference, apparently." His scrutiny was making her heart malfunction again, flushing excess heat into her cheeks.

"Not enough? Why? You mean because I recognized you?"

She shrugged. "You did—instantly."

"Not quite instantly." His smile hovered. "Don't let that worry you. I was trained to be observant."

"Oh?" she asked, interested. She'd been taught to observe people, too, or thought she had. "Why?"

His smile vanished; his features seemed to sharpen and solidify, like a picture coming into focus. For a moment, then, Tannis saw the derelict's face again. The dark side . . .

With a curious lack of expression Dillon said, "I used to be a cop."

"A cop," Tannis said. "Oh, boy." She took a bite of her sandwich, chewed, and swallowed. "Where, here?"

He shook his head. "Los Angeles. Vice, mostly." He flicked the brim of his baseball cap and laughed, but his laughter had a hollow sound, like an old newspaper blowing down an empty street. "I've spent a lot of time in getups like this, working undercover on downtown streets."

Tannis had a very graphic imagination. The series of images it projected in her mind took away her appetite. Staring down at the sandwich in her hands, she swallowed and murmured, "I guess by comparison Los Padres must seem—"

"Like a nursery school playground," Dillon confirmed flatly, looking at her, then away.

Tannis knew then that she'd been right; Dillon James knew the darkness well. He'd lived in it. And it had left its mark on him.

She heard the husky whisper of a sigh as Dillon shook off the shadows, pulling the cap from his head and raking his fingers through his hair, trying to catch whatever breeze might be passing. His hair looked clean, and captured the sun in reddish highlights. As she watched him, Tannis felt the fingers of her right hand curl with an unexpected but undeniable desire to comb her fingers through his hair, smoothing it away from his forehead. Discomfited, she looked at the offending hand with reproach and rubbed it against her thigh.

When he was finished with his sandwich, Dillon stretched and draped his arms across the top of the park bench. As he lifted his hand to give the pompon on Tannis's cap a lazy tug, his smile appeared like the sun from behind a windblown cloud. "This must be hot. Why don't you take it off?"

Tannis clapped her hand over the cap and shook her head. Swallowing a bite of her own sandwich suddenly became very difficult. "I'd have to take the wig off too."

"Well? Why not?"

She looked at him, unable to explain to herself or him why the act of taking off her wig in front of him seemed so frighteningly intimate. Improvising, she said, "Somebody might see me."

"Ah. The street people, you mean." Dillon frowned and sat forward, clasping his hands together between his knees. In an abrupt change of mood he asked bluntly, "Tannis, how long have you been living on the streets without backup?"

"Backup?" She smiled at the term. "Now you sound like a cop. Oh, wow, do you have any idea how foolish I feel? Accusing you of observing from your ivory tower, challenging you to come down and see how things *really are*"— she lifted two fingers on each hand, enclosing her words in mocking quotes—"when all the time—"

"It wasn't my intention to make you feel foolish," Dillon said, clipping his words impatiently. "And you haven't answered my question."

He looked so grim that Tannis drew away from him a little. Uncertain, not quite sure what he was getting at, she murmured, "Uh . . . well, I started *staying* out right after Thanksgiving—but I went home to my folks for Christmas."

"You went home for Christmas." Dillon dropped his

head into his hands, rubbing his eyes as if looking at her had become a strain. He muttered something under his breath, but all Tannis could make of it was the word *lucky*. He turned to give her a long, grave stare. "Hasn't anyone ever told you that what you're doing is dangerous?"

"Oh, sure." Tannis nodded. "Everybody has—more than once."

"Everybody?"

"Well, everybody who knows about what I'm doing. My sister and brother-in-law, Gunner, and now you."

"But you didn't believe them?"

"Of course I believed them!"

"No," Dillon said very quietly, "I really don't think you did. I don't think you realize that for every hard luck case and quaint character you've met on the street there's probably a dozen representatives of every kind of sociopathology imaginable. I'm talking about people who live in a world populated by demons, people without even the tiniest scrap of conscience, people who've fried their brains on drugs you've probably never heard of. I still don't think you have a clue, Tannis, not even after the scare I gave you."

"I'm a psychologist," she said evenly. "I'm not as innocent of the human condition as you seem to think I am. And anyway"—she straightened her back and looked pointedly at the squiggle of dried blood on his temple—"I think I'm capable of defending myself."

Dillon snorted.

Tannis stood up and dropped the uneaten half of her submarine sandwich back into the bag. Fighting to control her temper, she shoved the sleeves of her sweater above her elbows, paced a few steps, then turned to look down at him, hugging herself. "You know," she said quietly, "you could probably screw this up for me if you wanted to. You probably have the authority to keep me from completing my research, or at the very least, to make it difficult for me. But this means a lot to me, and if you keep me from doing my research here, I'll just have to go somewhere else. I chose this town because my sister lives here, but there are other places that will do as well." She paused. "I can always go to L.A."

Dillon leaned back and glared up at her with eyes as hard and cold as diamonds. "The hell you will!" Tannis glared back at him, breathing hard, puzzled by the intensity of his reaction. After a moment he shook his head and leaned forward again. So quietly she could barely hear him above the distant din of city traffic, he said, "Tannis, I don't want you to stop what you're doing. I just want you to stop doing it alone." He got to his feet and looked down at her, his thumbs hooked in the pockets of his ragged jeans. "I have a proposition for you. I want you to work for me. And with me."

As she so often did when he stood near her like that, Tannis felt overwhelmed. Not liking the feeling, she put her hand out and stepped back, a defensive movement designed to put a comfort zone between them. "Work . . . for you?" she said, incredulous. "Doing what?"

His gaze rested on her face. She felt it warm and soften until it seemed almost like a caress.

"Tannis, I told you I care about the problems of the homeless in this town, and that's a pretty big understatement. It was one of the issues I campaigned on, and since the election I've made it a personal goal to do something about it. When I decided to tackle this thing, I knew I had to get back to the streets to find the answers, but I've been away from them too long. It's beginning to look like I'm not going to have the time to reacclimate myself. Something needs to be done now. It'll take me weeks to develop the kind of rapport you already have. If you were to work with me, we might just come up with some solution—something a lot better than what's going on right now. What do you say?"

What do you say? The excitement she felt over Dillon's surprising proposition was becoming lost in a fog of other emotions. She had a panicky feeling, as if she'd suddenly lost her train of thought in mid-sentence. She couldn't concentrate. All of a sudden there didn't seem to be room in her mind for anything but Dillon's face, Dillon's voice. . . .

When she just stared at him, he added softly, "I won't get in the way of your personal research, I promise. And you'd be helping your street friends at the same time. Will you at least think it over?"

"Oh, yes," Tannis whispered.

"You will? You'll think about it?"

She cleared her throat and heard herself say, "No. I mean, I don't need to think about it. I'll do it. I'll be . . . delighted to work with you. It would be—"

"Hey, that's great!" His smile illuminated his face as he caught her up in an impulsive hug. Her heart gave a joyous surge; she clutched his arms and sucked in air like a child on a Ferris wheel.

"Hey," she said feebly, laughing, "don't you think this looks a little funny?"

"Oh," Dillon said. "Yeah." He dropped his arms and backed away from her. Suddenly it seemed that neither of them knew quite what to do with their hands or eyes. Dillon dragged his hands through the air while Tannis used hers to tug needlessly at the bottom of her sweater.

Dillon looked at his watch. "Uh, listen, I'd like to talk to you a lot more about this, share some ideas, make some plans, and so forth. But I have to be at a meeting at two, and I need to get home and change." His expression grew thoughtful, then enthusiastic. "You know, I'd really like to have you at that meeting. I'd like to make this official—get you on the city payroll."

"Payroll?" Tannis said, feeling breathless and overwhelmed. "You're offering me a job?"

He frowned. "Yeah, what did you think?" He picked up his baseball cap from the bench, slapped it once on his leg, and put it on. "Listen, tell you what. You take your time, go home, and get yourself cleaned up. I'll go to the meeting and you can join me there. That'll give me time to brief the mayor and the other members of the council. That okay with you?"

"Fine," Tannis murmured, spellbound.

He gave her a wide smile and reached impulsively toward her. Instead of touching her, though, he waved his hand and backed away. "Great . . . see you then." He turned, and she saw his shoulders take on the derelict's slouch.

"Dillon?" He turned back expectantly. She hesitated, feeling confused, not sure why she'd called him back, knowing only that she didn't want to watch him walk away. "Can I ask you a question?"

"Sure, shoot."

"How *did* you know me? What, exactly, was it that gave me away?"

He walked back to her, in no great hurry, thumbs hooked in his pockets . . . an unconscious but blatantly masculine swagger. She sensed the sultry throb of drums growing steadily louder and more hypnotic with every step he took.

"What gave you away?" His voice had a new timbre, warm and velvety, like a summer night.

He stood looking down at her, and though she felt as overpowered as she usually did by his height, this time she didn't retreat to her zone of comfort. Instead, she stood her ground, and discovered to her surprise and dismay that feeling overpowered wasn't necessarily unpleasant.

"It's your eyes," Dillon said, touching her with his gaze. She'd never known so compelling a touch; she felt it with every nerve cell in her body; she felt as if she couldn't move, or think, or even breathe without its guidance. "Your eyes give you away. . . ."

He didn't say anything more, but the world of sounds all around them retreated. City noises . . . horns honking, a jet plane's drone, the muted roar of traffic, a distant siren; park noises . . . laughter, voices, the skirl of skateboards, a barking dog. Tannis heard none of it. She stood very still, her hands at her sides clutching faded cotton, wrinkling it beyond redemption. Her ears were full of the sounds of her own heartbeat, her own breathing, and a tiny inner voice shouting warnings.

His soft chuckle was like a rock hurled through a window, letting in the noise along with cold, fresh air. Tannis released her breath in a faint gasp. "My eyes?"

"Yeah. You know what they say about eyes being windows of the soul? Yours had too much passion in them . . . too much fire. You forgot to hide them." He was moving away now, lifting his hand to the brim of his cap in a little salute that both apologized and gently chided.

Tannis whispered, "Ohh," and watched him move away in the derelict's shambling walk and blend with the crowd near the Spanish fountain.

Five

"A committee?" Mayor Flintridge said, frowning.

The silence in the meeting room was broken by the faint percussion of the mayor's fingertips meeting the tabletop.

Dillon cleared his throat. He was feeling his way through this, too new at politics to be able to do anything except trust his instincts. "A panel, actually. Made up of people with special knowledge and awareness of the problems of the homeless." There, he thought; that sounded sufficiently glib and ambiguous.

"Such as?"

"Well," he said, still cautious, "representatives of the city and law enforcement, and the service organizations—Salvation Army, Red Cross, et cetera. And I think for such a panel to be effective, it would almost have to include someone from the street community."

"Uh-huh," the mayor said thoughtfully tapping his teeth with a pencil.

Encouraged, Dillon leaned forward and clasped his hands together on the tabletop. "As you know, I have quite a bit of personal experience along these lines myself—"

The mayor snorted. "Some pretty recent."

There were sounds from the others present at the conference table that could only be called titters. Dillon grinned. "I'd be happy to chair the committee, George, and, of course, as mayor you'd automatically be a member." He paused. "In addition, I'd like to propose that we consider hiring a part-time consultant."

"You want to hire somebody?" The mayor was frowning again. "I was under the impression you were talking about a volunteer committee. We're not budgeted—"

"We're budgeted for staff. I haven't hired a secretary yet. I'm proposing instead to hire a part-time assistant to work with me on this. To act as a special liaison with the street people."

There was a murmur of comment around the table. The mayor drawled, "Liaison . . . Well, if that means that our junior member intends to stay out of the streets himself from now on— "

"Not to mention out of jail," Logan muttered. The other council members snickered. Dillon kept his mouth shut.

"I don't see any objection to hiring somebody," the mayor continued, looking expansive. Dillon could see him visualizing headlines in his mind already. MAYOR HIRES EXPERT TO STUDY HOMELESS PROBLEM! "Although I don't know where you're going to find—"

"Actually," Dillon broke in hurriedly, "as it happens, I've already spoken to a social psychologist with special knowledge and, ah, experience dealing with the homeless. As a matter of fact, I've asked her to come to this meeting." He checked his watch. "She should be here any minute."

Another ripple went around the table. Under cover of it Logan leaned over and muttered out of the corner of his mouth, "*She*? I think I'm beginning to get the picture."

Dillon gave him a quelling glare.

"What in the dickens," the mayor asked peevishly, "is a social psychologist?"

"Ah . . . well, I believe she's got degrees in both soci-ology and psychology, and is currently working on her Ph.D. in one or the other. I'm sure you'll be impressed with her when you meet her."

"I can hardly wait," Logan said, his eyes gleaming.

Dillon glanced at his best buddy, wondering how he could manage to throttle him in front of four witnesses. Maude Harrington was already hiding a smile behind her hand; obviously, Dillon's reputation as one of Los Padres's more visible bachelors hadn't gone unremarked in the powder rooms of City Hall.

"Ms. Winter is a professional—" he began, and was brought to a halt by sounds of a loud altercation com-ing from the reception area.

Fred Gould, who liked to tilt his chair back during informal meetings like these, muttered, "Jeez, what's that?" and righted himself with a thump. Somebody else said, "What the hell—?"

The mayor leapt to his feet.

There was the clamor of arguing voices and some muffled bumps and scuffles. Logan stood up and casu-ally reached a hand inside his jacket.

"Here—ma'am—please, you can't go in there!" The door to the meeting room burst open, admitting Tannis, resplendent in her shapeless tweed coat and purple pompon. Sally the receptionist followed, looking wild-eyed and harried.

The mayor bellowed, "Who the *hell* is this?"

Dillon jumped up just in time to intercept Logan, who already had Tannis's arm in a no-nonsense grip. Muttering "Uh . . . buddy, I'll take it from here," he claimed Tannis's arm while he tried to calm Sally with an apologetic smile. To Tannis he said, "What's going on? I thought you were going to change."

"Sorry," she whispered back, peering up at him through a pair of green-tinted rimless glasses as thick as Coke bottles. Behind them her eyes looked enor-mous, and slightly demented. "I didn't have time to go home and change. I bought these glasses instead. What do you think—do they do the trick?"

Dillon thought she looked like a giant, tattered moth. "Your own mother wouldn't recognize you," he whispered, amazed at how disappointed he was. Until that moment he hadn't realized how much he'd been looking forward to seeing her again. Her—Tannis—looking the way she'd looked in his office this morning. He was beginning to wonder if he'd dreamed that lovely, vibrant woman with the mane of sun-shot hair. . . .

"Dillon," the mayor said with ominous calm, "I take it this is your 'representative of the street community'?"

Exhaling slowly through his nose, Dillon turned to face his colleagues. Only George Flintridge was looking at him; the others were all staring at Tannis with varying degrees of horror and fascination. "George," he said grimly, "fellow council members and, uh, friends." He glanced at Logan, whose eyes, above the hand covering the lower part of his face, were suspiciously bright. "I'd like to have you meet Tannis Winter. The, uh, social psychologist I was just telling you about. Tannis, Mayor Flintridge . . ."

"Pleased to meet you, sir," Tannis said politely, thrusting out a gloved hand. Flintridge regarded it the way a sane man would the head of a cobra, and then, probably in a state of shock, took it anyway and gave it a shake. Slowly the other members of the city council followed suit.

"Ms. Winter," the mayor said severely, "would you mind explaining this . . . ?" He waved his hand to take in her general appearance.

"Not at all." Giving Dillon a look he couldn't even begin to read, thanks to the blasted glasses, Tannis shuffled to a position near the foot of the conference table, where she could command all eyes—not that anyone present would have considered looking anywhere else. Her voice was her own but one Dillon hadn't heard before. Calm, cool, completely in control. He couldn't help but admire her, which frustrated him even more.

"For several weeks I have been living on the streets of this city, dressed pretty much the way I am now. That's where I met Dillon—Mr. James—although I didn't know it was him at the time." She paused to throw Dillon an impish look that probably would have been irresistible on her own face, then turned abruptly serious.

"This morning I came to these offices to see you, Mayor Flintridge. I came as a concerned citizen—as myself—to discuss the problems of the homeless as I have become familiar with them firsthand. You were not available, so I was shown to Mr. James's office instead. I was treated with every courtesy, and a measure of respect." She paused to take a breath. "A few moments ago, visiting these same offices for much the same purpose, invited, this time, I was denied entry, threatened with eviction, manhandled"—she threw Logan an accusing look which he returned with an unabashed and wholly appreciative grin—"and in general treated like an unpleasant smell." She glanced around the conference table. No one spoke.

"The only difference I can see," she went on quietly, "is in the way I look. You have a well-publicized 'open door' policy, Mr. Mayor, but because I look like a 'street person,' your door was *not* open to me. And that, gentlemen, ma'am"—she nodded at Maude Harrington—" is my point. Street people are often treated as if they have no rights at all. And yet they are citizens of this city, just as you are. As I am." She glanced again at Dillon, and this time he saw a faint but unmistakable flush stain her cheeks. Looking quickly back at the mayor, she went on in a low, hurried voice. "I apologize for causing a commotion, but I seem to have pointed up one of the biggest problems the homeless face. First and foremost, we must not forget that these are human beings. Their individual rights must not be violated in the process of . . ." She hesitated, looked once more at Dillon, took a deep breath, and blurted out, "polishing up this city's image for the purposes of political and financial gain!"

There was a faint gasp from somewhere, quickly stifled. Dillon put his hand over his eyes. And then, morbidly fascinated, he opened his fingers and stole a peek at the mayor.

But George Flintridge had dealt with tougher adversaries than Tannis Winter. Leaning forward, the canny old politician adopted an expression that reminded Dillon of a school principal addressing a miscreant—stern, and a little disappointed.

"Ms. Winter," he said softly, "I do appreciate your concern. But let me remind you of one thing, young lady. I have been a member of this town's council since you were in diapers, and in every one of those years there have been people sleeping in its streets. Of course, in those days we called them bums and vagrants—we're more enlightened now. But the problem of homeless people isn't new, and it isn't going to go away, not today, not tomorrow, and not because you are here to champion the cause. It's a problem that's so big and so complex, there aren't any easy answers. They don't exist. The plain truth is, there isn't a lot we as a city can do. I am well aware that these people need more than a bed, a shower, and a square meal. They need low-cost housing, they need jobs, and, in most cases, some sort of counseling. We simply don't have the resources—the money."

The mayor filled his lungs, drawing himself up to his best public-address posture. Even Dillon had to admit he was impressive. "But there is one thing I can do, young lady, and that's see that the citizens of this city, and its guests, at least don't have to look at cardboard box shantytowns in its streets and alleys. I can make it so that people can walk down our streets without stepping in filth, or over the legs of people sleeping in doorways. I can't do much, Ms. Winter, but, by God, I will do what I can!"

There was a weighty silence. Dillon switched his fascinated gaze to Tannis and saw that though the flush in her cheeks had deepened, the eyes behind the ghastly glasses were unwavering. His admiration for her grew.

"Mr. Mayor," Tannis said evenly, "I appreciate your problem as well as your sincere efforts to solve it. If I can come up with better alternatives, would you be willing to listen to them?"

Another silence. The mayor pursed his lips, then leaned back and smiled benignly. "I would, indeed. Of course I would. And I think I can safely speak for the council on that subject. We all want to do the best we can for all our citizens. And now, Ms. Winter, if you'll excuse us, I believe Councilman James has a proposal we need to vote on."

Tannis swallowed, nodded, and shuffled toward the door. Logan jumped up to open it for her. Dillon coughed, muttering, "Think I'd better abstain; let me know what you decide," and went after her.

She'd stopped just outside the meeting room door. Dillon almost ran into her, and caught her by the arms to steady himself. Even through all the layers she was wearing he could feel her body shaking.

"I'm sorry," she said, sounding out of breath. "Did I mess things up?"

Dillon shook his head. "I don't know. I guess we'll find out in a minute."

"I don't know what got into me. I really shouldn't have said that about image, and political gain."

"It's okay. It needed to be said. I just wish I'd had the courage."

"Then . . . you aren't angry?"

"Angry?" Dillon stared at her, frowning. His hands still gripped her arms; now his thumbs began to stroke the rough fabric of her coat. He was really beginning to hate that coat.

"You looked angry, in there . . . when I walked in."

Remembering his disappointment and frustration

with the way she looked, Dillon said softly, "I wasn't angry." He watched her tongue run lightly across the surface of her lips, and noticed again that her upper lip was uneven, slightly irregular in shape. It gave her mouth a piquant quality he found very provocative.

She was saying, "I got to thinking about what you said about my eyes, and I realized you were right—I did need to disguise my eyes. So I went to this novelty place over on Fifth, and I found these. I just love them. Aren't they great?"

"Terrific," Dillon said. She gave a small gasp of surprise when his fingers touched her face, and he lifted the glasses from her nose. "There," he stated, "that's better." Her winter-bright eyes stared up at him. He saw confusion in them. He tried to explain, but all he could say, an unfamiliar roughness in his voice, was, "You don't need to hide them from me."

The sounds of their breathing filled the silence. Dillon's hands settled on Tannis's shoulders, and he felt the vibrations of heat and energy coursing through her body. His fingers tightened.

The door to the meeting room opened.

"Approved," Logan announced, closing the door and leaning against it. "Unanimously."

Dillon stared down into Tannis's face. It came as a shock to him to see a wrinkled old lady. Except for those eyes, of course, looking back at him with cold fires in their depths, reminding him that underneath the makeup and rubber wrinkles her skin was as fine-grained as silk and dusted with cinnamon freckles. Reminding him that under the layers and layers of cloth in his hands there was a young woman's taut, healthy body, and that inside the gloves that were clutching the sleeves of his jacket there was a pair of hands whose touch he'd once felt on his forehead as fleetingly and enchantingly as a chaste kiss.

"Hey, buddy, did you hear what I said? They've given you the green light."

Dillon exhaled softly and forced his stiff fingers to relax. Tannis slipped slowly out of his grasp.

"That's great," Dillon said, forcing a smile for the benefit of Logan's interested appraisal. His heart was beating as if he'd just run up a few flights of stairs.

"Yes, great," Tannis echoed. Even with all the makeup on she looked flushed. There was a little silence, during which Logan looked from Dillon to Tannis and back again. Dillon wished he'd go away.

"Well," Tannis said after a moment with a laugh and a shrug, "where do we go from here?"

Good question, Dillon thought. At the moment he wasn't sure just where he and Tannis were going, but he had a feeling it might be a lot further than either of them had expected.

"We hit the streets," he said, dragging himself back to the business at hand. "The first thing I'd like to do is meet some of these friends of yours."

"Sure. Right now?"

Logan said, "Uh . . . buddy," and jerked his head toward the conference room door.

"Right—the meeting. I guess this'll have to wait until tomorrow. Tell you what. You come to my office in the morning—there's going to be some paperwork to take care of anyway—and we'll leave from there."

"Dressed like this?" Tannis asked, the smile in her eyes crinkling the latex around them like old tissue paper.

"Yes," Dillon said reluctantly, "dressed like that." He held out the glasses. He noticed that she accepted them gingerly, careful not to touch his hand in the process.

"Okay then . . . see you tomorrow." Her voice had that breathlessness again.

"Yeah . . . take care now."

"Bye. . . ."

"Interesting lady," Logan said under his breath as they watched Tannis's shuffling progress down the long hallway. "I gotta tell you, though, your tastes sure have changed."

Dillon turned to scowl at him. "What are you talking about?"

"I'm talking about the fact that if I'd been a couple seconds later interruptin' you two, I'd have gotten the shock of my life, that's what."

"Come on, Logan."

"You aren't going to try to tell me you weren't just about to kiss her?"

Dillon snorted irritably. "For Pete's sake, she looks like Ma Kettle."

"My point exactly."

Dillon glared, then burst out laughing. "She doesn't really look like that. You ought to see her without all the makeup. She's really something. You wouldn't recognize her."

"I guess I'll have to take your word for it," Logan drawled as he pushed open the conference room door. "Otherwise, I'm gonna have to start worryin' about you."

"Next time I get her out of the makeup, I'll introduce you," Dillon whispered. But as he took his seat at the table he was frowning again, and feeling a little bit wistful. There were quite a few things he'd like to do with Tannis if he could just get her out of that bag lady's disguise. But at the moment he couldn't think how he was going to accomplish that.

Going down in the elevator, Tannis ignored the stares of two teenagers holding traffic citations and a woman in a janitor's uniform. She took off her glasses and carefully wiped her eyes on her coat sleeve.

She was shaken.

She could still feel the weight of Dillon's hands on her shoulders. She could still feel the rigid muscles of his forearms under the soft wool fabric of his jacket, muscles that had been rawhide tough and quivering with reserves of strength and self-control.

She was remembering the first time he'd touched her, out there on the street, when she'd thought he was a homeless derelict. When she'd first felt the attraction and found it so unsettling, she'd run from it, and from him.

It was different now. He wasn't a derelict after all, but a very charismatic and entirely eligible city councilman. Why did she still feel so shaken by his touch that her legs were trembling?

He'd wanted to kiss her. She'd felt it in the rigid muscles beneath the soft wool fabric of his coat sleeves, and she'd seen it in his eyes. Tannis had been kissed enough times in her life that she had no trouble at all recognizing that look.

How could he! she thought, making a little sound of astonishment that drew a wary glance from the janitor. How could he want to kiss her when she looked like . . . what she looked like!

Oh, but if he had . . . Just for a moment she let herself think about kissing Dillon. It wouldn't be a polite hello, a tentative exploration, a gentle quest. No, she thought, kissing Dillon would be like jumping off the high diving board—dangerous, exciting, a heart-stopping plunge into deep waters, with no turning back. . . .

"Wow, two nights in a row," Lisa said, coming out to the garage as Tannis was stripping off the last layer of socks. "What's wrong? Did you run into that guy again?"

"No," Tannis said with a soft, ironic laugh. "Not exactly. Well, sort of."

"That definitely clears that up. Are you going to get right into the shower? Do you want anything to eat? How about some coffee?"

"Coffee would be great. Thanks."

As she fished a crumpled pair of sweats out of the

dryer, Tannis thought for the thousandth time about how lucky she was to have a sister like Lisa. They'd always been so close—best friends, really—in spite of the differences between them. In fact, they were so different, sometimes Tannis wondered how they could even be sisters. Though when they were very small, strangers had often taken them for twins, understandable since there was only fifteen months difference in their ages, and in those days their coloring had been almost identical. Two adorable little blond, blue-eyed pixies, as different as day and night . . .

Day and night. *Dark and light.* And just like that, she was thinking of Dillon again.

In the kitchen Lisa was sitting at the table with a cup of steaming coffee between her hands. Tannis went to her and put her arms around her from behind.

"Oh, Lisa," she said with a sigh, "sometimes I envy you."

Her sister looked up in surprise. "*You* envy *me*? For heaven's sake, why?"

"I don't know. You just always know what you want. Even when we were kids you were always so stable, so even-tempered and unselfish. And I was *always* in trouble. I threw temper tantrums, I was naughty and disobedient, my room was a catastrophe, and I used your things without asking. How could you have put up with me?"

"What in the world is *this* mood?" Lisa said, laughing. "You envied me? Tannis, I was klutzy and shy. You were funny and exciting, and you thought up the most marvelous adventures—"

"Which always ended in disaster!"

"And without which my childhood would have been boring as hell. You were the one having a wonderful time. You were the one with all the boyfriends! Remember that time you told me you and your roommates in college decided to see if you could remember all the boys you'd ever kissed? And you made a list and counted them up, and you won, hands down! I couldn't believe how many—something like fif—"

"Lisa!" Tannis had a hand over her eyes. "Please, don't remind me!"

"And I didn't even date until halfway through college!"

"And then," Tannis said softly, "you met Richard."

"Yes." Lisa smiled. "I met Richard."

"First time out, you come up with a prince. I've kissed a zillion frogs, and I'm still looking. And here you are, doing what you were always meant to do, happily-ever-aftering in your beautiful house with your beautiful husband and beautiful, wonderful child. Every woman's dream . . ."

"Not every woman's," Lisa reminded her. "Not yours."

"No," Tannis emphatically agreed, "not mine."

"But, Tannis, aren't you doing what you always wanted to do?" The little lines of concern had appeared between Lisa's eyes. "I mean, you had so many wonderful and exciting things you wanted to do. And you've done them! There was that year you spent in Europe, and then acting school in New York, and then U.C.L.A. and all those degrees. And pretty soon you'll have your Ph.D., and you'll be *Doctor* Winter!"

"Yes," Tannis said, "that's true."

"You are happy, aren't you? I mean, you never wanted any of this." She waved a hand, taking in the cheerful kitchen, the house and yard, the whole neighborhood beyond. "I remember when we were little and you used to pretend you were in jail and the pickets on the fence around our yard were the bars. Remember that? I always thought that's the way it really felt to you."

Tannis nodded. "It did. I could hardly wait to get out into the big, wide, wonderful world."

"And then there was what you said to me when I was pregnant. You said children weren't for you because children started with a big c-h, as in chains."

"Good Lord," Tannis said, laughing. "I'd forgotten. What a terrible thing to say."

Lisa shook her head. "Not for you. You were probably right. I know you love Josh, and you're a wonderful aunt, but I can't see you as a mother, Tannis, at least not for a long time yet. There's just so much you want to do.'

"Yes," Tannis said, sighing.

They sipped coffee in silence. The cuckoo clock Tannis had sent from Germany ticked loudly.

Tannis got up from the table, placed her coffee cup carefully in the sink, and ran water into it. She turned the water off, wiped her hands on a towel, took a deep breath, and faced her sister. "I met a city councilman today—the new one."

"Dillon James?" Lisa's eyebrows shot up. "I've met him! A friend of mine gave a coffee for him during the campaign. Oh, Tannis—" Her voice dropped an octave. "He's a *very* dynamic man."

"He offered me a job."

"He what? That's wonderful! Doing what? You accepted, didn't you?"

"I did. I could hardly refuse. He offered me a chance to work with him on this homeless thing." She paused to take a deep breath. Lisa shook her head in a confused sort of way.

"Tannis, what's wrong with this picture? Why aren't you crowing with delight? This sounds like a great opportunity for you, and besides, he's very attractive."

"Too attractive," Tannis said in a low voice. "So attractive he scares me."

"Oh, Tan, I don't believe this. You? You're like a kid in a candy store when it comes to men! I mean, you like men. You're always so . . . at ease with them. You must have dated a hundred guys, and you thought they were all wonderful, and they're all your friends and still think the world of you. And they were all attractive. You've never been intimidated by an attractive man in your life. So what is this?"

"I didn't mean it like that. I mean—" Hugging herself, she rubbed at her arms, which had suddenly acquired a rash of goose bumps. "I don't think I've ever been this attracted to a man," she said in a low voice. "I think . . . I could really get to like him. Really like him, you know?"

"So? What's wrong with that? You were just complaining about all the frogs you've kissed. Maybe it's about time you found that prince."

Tannis abruptly turned her back on her sister and gripped the edge of the sink. Facing her dim reflection in the window, she could manage to control the threatening pressure in her throat. "Lisa?" She paused, swallowed, took a deep breath, and went on. "You know that kissing thing you were talking about? Where we all counted up and I won? Well . . . what I didn't tell anyone—mainly because I didn't think anybody would believe me—was that I was also, um, a virgin."

"Oh," Lisa said readily, "I believe it."

Tannis turned an incredulous look on her. "You do? Why?"

Lisa shrugged. "It makes all kinds of sense. Unless you have some sort of emotional problem, you're not going to sleep with a guy until you get to know him pretty well, right? At least, I know *you* wouldn't, because that's the way you are. So, since you never dated anybody long enough to get to know him well—except for Dan, of course . . . She paused. "Not even with Dan?"

Tannis turned back to the sink just in time to hide an involuntary spasm of pain. "Nope," she said neutrally. "Not even Dan." *Not then.* Not until much, much later—but that was something too painful to tell anybody, even Lisa. No one would ever know about Dan.

"That's funny," Lisa mused. "I always had an idea you really did love Dan."

"I did," Tannis said, still keeping her voice smooth and light. "But the timing was wrong. I was too young, and there were so many things I wanted to do. I just couldn't let myself get serious with anybody, you know?" She tossed her head determinedly. "I still have too much to do—exciting things, important things. I've got to finish my research and get busy writing my paper so I can get my degree and get a real job."

"And then?" Lisa asked, coming to put her cup in the sink. "Will it be time for a serious relationship then?"

Tannis shrugged. "Maybe."

Her sister put her arms around her and hugged her. "Don't wait too long, Tan," she whispered huskily. "The longer you keep people at a distance, the more it gets to be a habit. If you've never let yourself be intimate, really close to someone, the idea can be pretty scary."

Or if the one time you do let someone get close, you get burned . . . But Tannis didn't say that out loud; that was one thing she'd never tell a living soul.

She had everything she needed, she told herself. Her life was rich, full, exciting, challenging. She had a million friends and a terrific family who gave her all the love in the world. She didn't need, or have time, to fall in love. *Not now.*

Six

The headline in the morning edition of the *Los Padres Daily Bulletin* read: MAYOR'S PANEL TO TACKLE HOMELESS PROBLEMS.

Well, Dillon thought, he hadn't been too far off.

"Mornin', Councilman. That be all for you?"

Dillon looked appraisingly at the man on the other side of the newsstand's counter. A big man, balding but somehow ageless. Massive shoulders and bulging muscles strained the seams of the olive drab long-sleeved shirt he wore half buttoned over a white cotton T-shirt. His neck rose from the collar of his shirt like the trunk of a tree. From the waist up, Dillon thought, he looked like a man who could bench-press a Mack truck. And in spite of the fact that the lower half of his body ended at mid-thigh, his eyes had the serenity of a quiet pond.

"How'd you know who I was?" Dillon asked curiously as he dug in his pocket for a quarter.

The man's chuckle was soft, a warm, rich sound. "Oh, I have my ways, Councilman. I have my ways." He tapped a stack of newspapers. Dillon grinned. The man held out his hand. "Gunner," he said as Dillon shook it. "Good to meet you, Mr. James."

"Dillon. Actually, I believe I know a friend of yours."

"Yeah?" Gunner glanced toward the other end of the counter, where a man in a herringbone tweed jacket was helping himself to a paper. "Mornin', your honor, how's it goin'?"

"Not bad, Gunner, not bad." The man flipped Gunner a quarter, which he caught with an effortless flick of the wrist.

"Thank you, sir, you take care now." He turned back to Dillon. "Friend of mine, you said?"

"Yeah," Dillon said. "Tannis Winter."

"Oh, yeah," Gunner said neutrally. "I know Tannis."

"I offered her a job," Dillon said, tapping the newspaper headline. "She's going to be working on this committee with me."

"Well, now," Gunner said, "that's nice. She'll like that. Right up her alley."

"Yeah," Dillon said, then turned his back to the counter. Leaning against the stand, he watched the passing traffic while Gunner took care of a couple of customers. He thought about Tannis, and the way he was beginning to feel about her, and when there was a lull, he dropped words into it without turning around.

"How long have you known her, Gunner?"

He heard the wheelchair's purr. "Awhile."

"She says you told her it's dangerous, what she's doing."

"I told her."

"To tell you the truth, Gunner, I'm worried about her. That's one reason why I offered her the job. She still hasn't got a clue how dangerous it is out there."

"No."

"She thinks she does."

Gunner nodded in agreement. "Her heart's in the right place."

"*You* know," Dillon said, finally turning to look at

Gunner and finding that quiet gaze resting on him in thoughtful appraisal.

"Yeah," Gunner said, "I know. And so do you."

There was a long silence, and then a smile ruffled the stillness of Gunner's eyes like a breeze stirring across calm waters. "She's tough though. Handles herself pretty well. Couple days ago I heard she banked a wino off a trash can and sank him right there in the gutter— smack in front of a cruising black-and-white. Sure wish I'd seen it."

Dillon grunted.

Gunner made change for an attractive woman in navy blue pinstripes who was buying copies of *Vogue* and *Computer World*. Together he and Dillon watched in appreciation as the woman stowed the magazines in her briefcase and went clicking off down the sidewalk, and then, still gazing at the passing crowd, Gunner said, "A wino's one thing. There's sharks and wolves out there, Councilman. You do me a favor, my friend. Keep an eye on her."

"I'll do that," Dillon said. He looked into Gunner's eyes and reached across the counter to take his hand in a hard grip. "Thanks . . . friend."

Tannis found Binnie sitting on a bus stop bench a block down from the Clifton Hotel, eating a sandwich. She almost didn't recognize her at first because she had on a new hat. This one was navy blue straw with some red and white flowers and berries on it. Tannis had seen hats just like it in department stores recently, though this one had obviously met with a major catastrophe before falling into Binnie's hands.

"Hi," she said, sitting down beside Binnie on the bench.

Binnie gave a startled jerk, smiled when she saw it was Tannis, then looked scared when she saw that she wasn't alone.

"It's okay," Tannis said, laying a reassuring hand on Binnie's arm. "This is my friend . . ."

"Dillon," he offered, shuffling forward. Binnie eyed him warily. Dillon took off his baseball cap and nodded at her. "That's a lovely hat you're wearing, ma'am."

Binnie's face broke into a smile. "Found it in the parking lot over at the shopping mall," she said gruffly. "Musta fell out of somebody's car. I think it got run over, but I don't know, I think it's got style. Of course," she added, looking doubtful for a moment, "it is a *spring* hat."

"Spring's on its way," Tannis assured her, looking up at Dillon, grateful and obscurely touched by the way he'd put Binnie at ease. The smile he gave her in return caused a funny little kick right under her ribs. She coughed and nudged Binnie. "Hey, we movin' uptown or something?"

Binnie made a face over her sandwich. "Hah—lost my spot. The cops came and made everybody leave."

"Yeah, I know." Tannis sighed.

Binnie looked at her, then craned up at Dillon. "You go to the shelter?" Dillon shook his head. "Nah," Binnie said, looking disgusted, "me, neither. I won't go to those shelters. Person can get mugged there. You know Crazy Frankie? Got beat up in a shelter last winter." She nodded sagely at Dillon. "Those shelters, they're worse than jail, you know that? I *know*. Oh, yeah, I been in jail. Shoplifting." She shrugged philosophically. "Well, shoot, it was a real bad week, and I was hungry. But the shelters? Same as jail—they spray you for bugs. That stuff causes cancer, you know that? And the worst of it is, they won't let you keep your stuff." She leaned close to Tannis and whispered, "They tell you it's because there's not enough room, but if you ask me, they keep it. Yeah . . . that's right! I know. Well, they ain't gonna get my things! I'm staying where I can keep an eye on 'em—it's the only way."

"You got a new place?" Tannis asked quickly to cover the strangled sound Dillon made.

Binnie shrugged. "Bunch of us been living down in the Ninth Street culvert. Know where that is? Clarence is there—he don't stay *in* the culvert, but he's down there. And Crazy Frankie, and The Showman . . . Hey, the cops cleaned out The Alley, you know that? Tore down all the boxes and tents and threw 'em in the dumpster. Good thing too—good riddance." Binnie shivered. "There was a lot of trash in The Alley—drugs. A lot of crazy, mean people. I was scared to go anywheres near that place. . . . Hey, you guys want some of my sandwich?"

Tannis shook her head, but Dillon stepped forward and said, "Sure . . . thanks." Tannis gazed at him as he accepted the sandwich and hungrily bit into it. If she hadn't known better, she'd have sworn it was the first decent mouthful of food he'd had all day.

How easily he does it, she thought in admiration.

Binnie grimaced when Dillon handed the sandwich back to her. "Yeah, I know—tuna fish." She shook her head. "I told the guy I was a vegetarian, and he brings me tuna fish. Probably shouldn't complain though. People sure have been nice today. Sure you don't want a bite? It's got alfalfa sprouts."

Tannis glanced up at Dillon, and again felt that odd little bump beneath her ribs. Distracted, she shook her head and stood up. "Think I'll go over to the culvert and see if I can find Clarence. You coming?"

Binnie shook her head. "I believe I'll just sit here in the sun a while longer. Arthritis," she explained matter-of-factly for Dillon's benefit. "Always gets bad when the nights turn cold."

"Where will she go?" Dillon asked as he fell into step beside Tannis's shopping cart.

Tannis shrugged and muttered, "She'll be okay. Binnie's been on the streets a long time." But she wished she felt better about it herself. Not that it was ever easy, but for some reason today she was having a hard time keeping any kind of clinical perspective at all. She thought it must have something to do with Dillon's presence. For some reason, being with him was making her feel . . . vulnerable. As if he'd barged into her heart and left the door open.

To fortify herself, she began to explain to Dillon about the Ninth Street culvert. Most east-west streets in the city deadended at Los Padres Creek; one of the few that didn't was Ninth Street, which happened to be a state highway. Where Ninth Street crossed the dry creekbed there was a culvert big enough to drive a pickup truck through.

"It's not a bad shelter," Tannis told Dillon. "The only trouble with it is that when it's most needed, it's not available."

Dillon laughed. "Yeah," he said, "I see what you mean." They were standing on the concrete bank of the dry wash that in rainy weather would be a raging torrent. "I would imagine that anybody desperate enough to sleep in that culvert this time of year sleeps with one eye on the sky."

Today, though, the skies were clear, and the wash had the look of an encampment. There were cardboard boxes and tattered mattresses on the floor of the culvert, and people lounging in the sun with their backs to the graffiti-covered concrete buttresses. Somebody even had a fire going in a ten-gallon bucket, the kind that had once held some sort of industrial goo.

Tannis found Clarence sitting about halfway up the side of the concrete embankment, the plastic trash bag that held all his worldly possessions tucked between his feet. He was a very thin man, with haunted, sunken eyes and shoulder-length hair that had probably once been blond. Like so many of the street people, it was impossible to guess his age. Poverty and hopelessness extract a much greater toll on both the body and the soul than time does, Tannis mused.

"Is this the high-water mark?" she asked, squatting down beside him.

"What the heck," Clarence said with a whimsical shrug, "it's been a dry year, but why take chances?" He squinted at Tannis. "Haven't seen you in a while. Thought maybe you'd gone to the shelter."

"Nope . . . been looking for you."

He shrugged again, looking apologetic. "I can't go to the shelter. I've tried, but—"

"I know," Tannis said, patting his hand. "It's okay." And then, softly she asked, "Clarence, have you eaten today?"

His smile was wistful. "Oh, I went over to the Rescue Mission last night. Guess I'll probably go again. They were okay about letting me stay outside, and the preaching's not that bad." He looked at Tannis. "You?"

It was Tannis's turn to shrug. "I'm doin' okay." Thinking of what Binnie had told her, she added, "Handouts have been pretty good since all the stuff about the homeless in the newspapers."

Clarence gave a dry chuckle. "Yeah, kind of jogs people's consciences, I guess. It'll pass." He looked away from her, down to where Dillon stood talking to The Showman and another man Tannis didn't know. After a moment he nodded toward the little group and said, "Who's the new guy?"

"Friend of mine," Tannis said. "Name's Dillon. He's okay." Clarence nodded and fell into one of his brooding silences while Tannis went on watching Dillon move among the mattresses and cardboard boxes below.

He's okay. Whatever it was about Dillon that had attracted her that very first morning was working its magic on the inhabitants of the wash. In bemusement Tannis watched him squat down to speak to Crazy Frankie, who was sitting on his mattress, muttering to himself. Frankie wouldn't answer, of course—he never did—and after a moment Dillon stood up and went to warm his hands over the fire in the bucket. Again

Tannis noticed how naturally he seemed to blend with the homeless people. It must come, she supposed, from all those years of experience as an undercover cop.

Cop. She'd forgotten about that. She had an idea that once a cop, always a cop at heart, and that could prove very awkward at her next stop. She didn't know how she was going to manage it, but somehow or other she was going to have to make that next stop alone.

"Ready to move on?" Dillon asked when she joined him down in the wash.

"I just remembered a couple of things I was supposed to do for my sister," Tannis told him, lying glibly. "Completely slipped my mind. Listen, why don't you stay here and get to know these people a bit more while I run my errands, and I'll meet you back at your office in . . . say, two hours?"

Dillon's eyes probed hers in a way that made shivers go up her spine, but he nodded and said simply, "Fine. See you later." And then, with the bracketed smile that always made a little pool of warmth inside her, he added, "Take care now. Just make sure you get there before dark."

"Right. I will." Feeling breathless and thoroughly dishonest, Tannis waved and began pushing her cart laboriously up the long incline that led to the street.

I wonder what she's up to, Dillon thought as he watched her go. Errands for her sister, my foot! It had been as patently clumsy a lie as he'd ever heard. He was a little amused by it, and a little disappointed too; he'd have liked to think she trusted him. Still, whatever she had in mind to do, it was obvious she wanted to do it without him tagging along, and he respected her right to privacy. When he set out to follow her, it wasn't because of any wish to invade that privacy but because suddenly he couldn't stand the thought of her walking alone through the bleak and lonely streets.

• • •

The vacant lot was one of those eyesores that seems to fall through the cracks of even the best intentioned bureaucracies. Adjacent to an abandoned garage and service station, it had at one time been the repository for the station's overflow of cars and parts. Now foxtail and tumbleweeds grew high and thick around the stripped-down car bodies and empty oil drums, the dry grass a seine that trapped windblown refuse like fish in a trawler's nets. It was a bleak place, reeking of failure and disillusionment. And to all appearances, except for Tannis and her shopping cart, it was deserted.

When a different movement caught the corner of Dillon's eye, he assumed it was just a cat hunting field mice in the weeds. Crouched in listening silence behind a half-stripped car abandoned in the street, he heard whispers, quickly shushed. And then, like nocturnal creatures emerging from their burrows at twilight, small, dark heads began to appear amid the jumble of scrap metal and junk.

Children. Dillon counted three, and then a girl who couldn't have been more than thirteen or fourteen, carrying a toddler. And finally a woman leading yet another child by the hand, calmly watching Tannis's approach with stoic pride in every line of her rail-thin body. Dillon heard the staccato sibilance of Spanish, soft ripples of irrepressible childish laughter, and repeated often and with excitement, the single syllable, "*Win . . .*"

Children. Of all the homeless, the plight of the children was the most intolerable. An old, familiar rage caught at Dillon's belly, writhing and twisting inside him, rising into his chest, hampering his breathing. It was such a helpless feeling, that rage against the injustices and cruelties of life. Fighting to control it, he closed his eyes and leaned his head against the car's rusty fender.

When he opened his eyes again, he saw Tannis take

a bag of groceries from its hiding place under the odds and ends in her cart and give it to the woman. Next came a plastic bag of oranges, which was immediately opened and its contents distributed among the children. They ate the fruit like voracious animals, devouring every bite, while Dillon watched, tasting his rage like acid in his throat.

Why hadn't she wanted him to know about this? He didn't understand it. Didn't she know he could help?

Tannis had been struggling with something tied to the handle of her cart. Finally, after pulling off a glove with her teeth, she managed to get it unfastened. Now she held it out to the woman in triumph—a pair of children's tennis shoes dangling from their laces. Dillon saw then that the child whose hand the woman held so tightly was barefooted.

It was too much for Dillon. Unable to look anymore, he sat on the pavement with his forearms resting on his drawn-up knees and his head back against the side of the car, fighting anger and the urge to jump out of his hiding place and get those kids into the hands of the Red Cross, or one of the county agencies. He kept telling himself to wait until he'd had a chance to ask Tannis what was going on. He kept telling himself she must have a reason for trying to keep this from him.

He waited until he heard the sounds of the cart and Tannis's shuffling footsteps going off down the sidewalk. When he finally crawled out of his hiding place, the vacant lot was once more, to all appearances, deserted.

As he followed the bobbing purple pompon through the crowded streets and lonely back alleys of Los Padres, Dillon did a lot of thinking about Tannis Winter, social psychologist, crusader, do-gooder, and, possibly, damn fool. She was a puzzle, and she was beginning to frustrate him terribly. He realized that the more he found out what kind of a person she was, the more he wanted to know her. And yet, in some indefinable way she seemed to keep him at a distance, putting up a thin but impregnable wall around her that he couldn't penetrate.

Like that blasted bag lady's makeup of hers. It was becoming unbelievably frustrating to him to realize that he'd still seen her only once without it. For those few tantalizing, bewitching minutes in his office, she'd been unguarded and open, both physically and emotionally. That meeting seemed distant and vague to him now, like a half-remembered dream. He wasn't certain whether he was beginning to forget or whether he was embellishing his memories, turning them into full-blown fantasies. He knew only that ever since then, seeing her in her disguise made him want to strip away the coat and wig, scrub off the makeup and latex wrinkles, and kiss her until the walls came tumbling down.

It was nearly dusk when Tannis entered the part of the city known to the street people as The Alley. The name had come to mean more than the alley itself; it referred now to the surrounding neighborhood as well. The actual alley bisected several blocks of squat brick buildings that housed an assortment of massage parlors, adult bookstores, bars and liquor stores, X-rated video stores and movie theaters. A few legitimate businesses still survived behind steel mesh and iron grids, catering to the people who lived in the decaying apartments above the stores. For the most part, the rent-paying residents tried to ignore their neighbors—the ones who spent the nights huddled in cardboard boxes and makeshift tents, and spent the days crouched on sunny sidewalks and in sheltered doorways, drinking, sleeping, and trading in drugs.

Partly because it nudged right against the back

doors of City Hall, and partly because it really was the heart of the city's skid row, The Alley had received the brunt of the mayor's clean-up campaign. As Binnie had said, the cardboard boxes and tents had been torn down and their occupants scattered. Now, though, just two days after the sweep, the former residents were already beginning to find their way back.

Tannis had been through The Alley before, of course, but never after dark. She hadn't meant to go there now, but time had speeded by her. She was already late meeting Dillon, and The Alley lay between her and City Hall.

The rattle and clank of her cart was disconcertingly loud on the nearly deserted sidewalk. Beneath that racket her shoes made a subdued accompaniment, a rhythmic swishing, like brushes on a snare drum. A few feet and a million light-years away in the street, expensive cars rushed by with locked doors and rolled-up windows, raising little whirlwinds of paper debris in the gutter. The streetlights came on, and shadows began to stir in nooks, crannies, and doorways.

Tannis walked quickly. Cold sweat misted her forehead and made tickling trails down her ribs. The hairs on her arms and the back of her neck lifted as if stirred by the breath of something unseen. Leaning against the cart, Tannis willed the swishing rhythm of her footsteps to an even faster tempo.

As she passed them, the shadows detached themselves from graffiti-covered walls to form a silent parade behind her, like alley cats following a fisherman.

I don't believe this, Tannis thought. This was danger, real and present. She was being stalked. She knew it, sensed it with every nerve and fiber in her being. In her mind she went over everything she'd been taught about self-defense, but her muscles felt weak and use-

less; she wondered whether adrenaline would come to her rescue when the time came.

Up ahead, a traffic light hung like a beacon. *Green.* Holding on to that calm, unwinking eye, Tannis pushed the cart faster and faster, praying all the while, *Don't turn red, please don't turn red. . . .*

Her prayer wasn't going to be answered. While she was still a few yards from the corner, the eye blinked yellow, and then red. Tannis halted, aware now that her heart was a thunder in her ears, her breathing a painful rasp in her dry throat. With a little sob of frustration she gripped the cart, prepared to cross with the traffic light even though it meant going out of her way. As she turned, one of the shadows that had been following her moved into the light, becoming a flesh and blood body in a denim jacket, and a dark face with hard, cold eyes. Another moved in close behind her, still a shadow, but with heat and density, and an unmistakable aura of menace.

A third shadow moved up beside her. When she felt the touch of a hand on her arm, all her muscles locked, and her mind went blank. She thought she might have made a sound, the kind small animals make when they feel the predator's claws.

"*It's me, you idiot!*" a voice whispered in her ear.

Light, hope, and understanding exploded through her, flooding her muscles with power and her heart with a wild, primitive joy. She looked up into Dillon's face and saw a wide, wolfish grin. There was a hard glitter in his dark eyes too.

The two young men who had been pursuing her looked at Dillon, and then at each other. They looked back at Dillon, who towered over both of them by at least a head. One of them gave a dry, mirthless chuckle and shrugged as if to say, *She's all yours, man.* They went slouching off down the sidewalk, nudging each other.

Tannis turned to say something to Dillon, but he

hissed at her under his breath and, grabbing her arm, forced her into a clumsy run. She lost both shoes in the middle of the street.

"Wait—my cart!" she gasped, but again Dillon hushed her with that wordless sibilance.

A block or so away Dillon finally paused to look back, allowing Tannis a chance to catch her breath and to ask again about her cart. She really hated to leave it behind.

"Your *cart*!" His eyes narrowed incredulously, and he gave his head a little shake, as if it needed clearing. And then Tannis saw his mouth lift sideways in his familiar half smile as he muttered under his breath, "I guess the Lord does protect children and fools."

Her mouth popped open, but before she could think of an answer to that, he grabbed her wrist again and took off down the street. She had no choice but to go with him.

"Ouch!" she cried as her stocking foot came down on something hard—a rock, probably. Hopping on one foot, she stumbled and nearly fell. Dillon stopped and looked at her for a moment, then muttered something under his breath and bent down to hook an arm behind her knees.

She gave a startled squawk as he hefted her—not gently—into his arms. "What are you doing?" she gasped. Her impulse was to struggle and demand to be put down immediately.

And then she looked at Dillon's dark face and swallowed further protests in one audible gulp. There was something about the set of his jaw, the gleam in his eyes, that made her heart go tripping helter-skelter through her chest like a child running too fast down a hill.

They were already crossing the street in front of City Hall. But instead of turning toward the lighted lobby, Dillon kept right on going through the parking lot and into the deserted park. Tannis cleared her throat, tapped him on the shoulder, and asked in a tone of mild curiosity, "Uh, Dillon, what are you doing?"

He looked down; his gaze swept slowly over her from the top of her purple cap to the toes of her baggy socks. "Something," he said vaguely. "Something I've been wanting to do."

Tannis stared at his angular profile while her imagination raced around in a vacuum. Where was he taking her? The slightly grim set of his smile made a shiver run through her. She could feel his pulse beating beneath her hands where they clung to his neck. She was suddenly aware of the enveloping heat of his body and of his heartbeat knocking against her side.

It occurred to Tannis suddenly that Dillon's progress across the park was not random; his path was arrow-straight and his footsteps firm with purpose. She also observed that he appeared to be heading straight for the Spanish fountain in the center of the park. A horrible thought struck her.

"You're not . . ." she squeaked, tightening her grip on his neck, "going to dump me in that thing?"

He gave a shout of laughter. The fountain gurgled and chuckled, sounding disgustingly merry. She felt its cool, misty kiss on her hot cheeks as Dillon's arms tightened around her. She gave a little gasp, closed her eyes, and wrapped her arms in a near stranglehold around Dillon's neck. In the next moment she felt her feet touch lightly down on the fountain's tile apron.

"You can let go of me now," Dillon said in a voice rich with laughter.

Tannis opened her eyes and found them about an inch from his stubbled chin. She blinked, and mumbled, "Oh." Relaxing her arms, she slipped them reluctantly from his neck. He caught them at the wrists and drew them down, out of his way, then reached for the buttons of her coat. She whispered, "What are you doing?"

"Taking your coat off."

"Why?" But by that time it was done. Dillon's hands slid upward, pushing the heavy coat over her shoulders. It fell with a slithery rustle and settled around her feet.

His hands felt warm on her shoulders, and warmer still on the bare skin of her neck. Her breath caught; awed and still, she felt his fingers burrow under the strands of her wig and lift both it and the cap from her head.

She gave a little gasp when she felt the coolness, and reflexively lifted her hands to her flattened hair. But Dillon's hands were there before hers; his fingers raked through her hair, discovering and discarding pins, unwinding the knot into which she'd twisted the golden strands to keep them out of sight under the wig. Her knees weakened unexpectedly. She grasped his wrists and felt the tendons in them surge and quiver like ropes against her fingertips. In a breaking voice she cried, "Dillon, what are you doing?"

"Something," he said softly, "that I've been wanting to do . . . ever since you walked into my office." One of his hands moved to support her head, curving warmly over the back of her neck. "Something you've been making pretty near impossible." The fingers of his other hand searched her face, quickly finding and stripping away the bits of molded latex.

With his hands still woven through her hair, Dillon drew her to the edge of the fountain. When he leaned over to scoop a handful of water from the fountain, she instinctively squeezed her eyes shut. Her mind had somehow stopped functioning. Except for one sharp gasp, she didn't move or protest when he began to wash her as if she were a child with a dirty face.

The water was cold, but Dillon's fingers were gentle. Tannis opened her eyes and stared up at him, enthralled by the feel of his fingertips on her cheekbones, the ball of his thumb sliding down the bridge of her nose, the hollow of his palm cupping her chin. She searched his face as he scrubbed at hers, disposing of the last vestiges of her makeup, while water dampened her collar, ran down her neck, and trickled into the hollow between her breasts.

She felt . . . confused.

"There now," he whispered, brushing her cheek with the backs of his fingers, "that's better." His body shifted; his face moved closer, then stopped. "Oops, not quite." His thumb skimmed lightly across her lower lip. "Open your mouth," he commanded softly.

And so completely was she under his spell that she complied. Dillon's water-chilled finger invaded her mouth, located and deftly disposed of the bits of padding that altered the shape of her face.

"*Now* . . ." he breathed, and pulled her into his arms.

Seven

It was as she had thought it would be—a plunge from the high board, dizzying, exhilarating . . . terrifying. She actually felt as if she were falling. Her heart and stomach surged upward, forcing an involuntary gasp from her throat. Tensing automatically, she clutched at Dillon's arms for support and found the muscles beneath her hands rigid. She felt the hardness of his body, the taut quivering deep inside him, like a just-released bow string.

For a moment, then, she felt overwhelmed, on the verge of panic. Again she found herself remembering the way she'd first seen him—as a derelict: darkly, dangerously, disturbingly attractive. Seeking reassurance, she lifted her hands to touch his face.

. . . And discovered, not a derelict, nothing dark or sinister, hard or cold, but only warm human flesh. A man's face. Dillon's face. She felt his skin, its rough and smooth places, its tiny irregularities. A day's growth of beard pricked her fingertips. She touched the grooves in his cheeks that so charmingly encompassed his smile.

And somewhere deep inside herself she felt another of those small explosions, and then a sweet, spreading warmth. With a sigh she relaxed and sagged against him.

Dillon's arms gentled around her; his mouth softened; his tongue traced and caressed her lips, then slipped between them and pressed deep in a slow and sensual merging, a tender penetration that seemed to cleave her body to its core. His legs shifted; one hand slipped down to stroke her lower back in easy, circling rhythms that coaxed her body against his. With his other hand he cradled the back of her neck, massaging upward into her scalp with his fingertips, bringing her head slowly to nestle in the curve of his broad shoulder.

Holding her thus, he claimed not only her mouth, he took possession of her entire body. It wasn't just a kiss, but a kind of erotic dance. With her eyes closed she seemed to whirl to its silent music and sway to the rhythms of her own body. He guided her so subtly and skillfully, she wasn't even aware that the rhythms weren't hers at all, but his.

Though if it was a dance, it was no civilized gavotte but something much more primitive that began slowly, like the throb of distant drums, and gradually increased in tempo and intensity until it filled her head with thunder and her body with heat. Her breath became heavy in her chest, so that at last she had to turn away, pulling her mouth from his with a desperate sound much like a whimper.

Dillon's breath expired in a warm gust against her cheek. For a few moments he held her there, his jaw pressed tightly to hers, while his fingers stroked sensuously at opposite ends of her spine, sending shock waves racing through her on collision course.

Her own hands, she discovered then, were holding on to Dillon's neck, and her fingers were burrowing through the hair that grew long on his nape. How warm his neck was, and how soft his hair, she thought; but beyond that she couldn't think at all. She didn't know what to say, didn't know what to do next, or even whether her legs would support her if he let her go.

And then, still holding her in that intimate embrace, Dillon began to chuckle. His body shook with it, rocking gently. It was soft laughter, easy laughter, a little embarrassed and more than a little surprised.

Also in need of some sort of emotional release, Tannis found herself laughing with him, pressing her forehead against his jaw.

"What was that all about?" she asked when at last he eased her away from him. She meant it to sound testy, but a certain hollowness and a touch of huskiness in her voice robbed it of conviction.

Dillon's hands rested on the rounds of her shoulders, absently kneading. His head was bent, and his eyes searched her face with dark intensity. "I'm not sure." He sounded bemused. "I don't think I meant to do that. I mean, I know I've been wanting to kiss you, just not . . ." His voice trailed off as he picked up a strand of her wet hair and rubbed it between his thumb and fingertips. "Not quite like this," he said with a soft, rueful laugh. "I didn't mean to do this to you."

"Well, then," Tannis said, delicately clearing her throat, "why did you?" It gave her an odd feeling to hear him admit to feeling as confused as she did. Excitement mixed with tenderness in her.

"I don't know." She saw his shoulders lift and expand with his indrawn breath, and then, with a smile in his voice, he said, "You've been frustrating the hell out of me, you know."

"Me? Why?"

There was silence while he stared down at her with his head bent, his face in shadow. Tannis stood still, forgetting to breathe while she tried to study his eyes. Unable to see them, she focused instead on his mouth . . . and remembered. She remembered with graphic immediacy the way his lips felt. She wanted to feel them again. Weakness flooded her, making her tremble.

"You're cold," Dillon said suddenly, harshly.

The suddenness of his withdrawal chilled her as the water had not. "Small wonder," she muttered, feeling dismal and rejected. "I'm all wet."

His voice was gentle, but he didn't move toward her or put his arms around her. "I know. I'm sorry about that." He bent to pick up her coat and dropped it over her shoulders. "Come on, my car's over in the City Hall lot. I'll take you home."

They said very little on the drive, except to ask and give directions. Dillon drove with one hand, keeping the other loosely arranged over the lower half of his face. His expression, in the intermittant illumination of street- and headlights, suggested deep and troubling thoughts.

Tannis kept her eyes straight ahead for the most part, and thought about how damp and itchy and uncomfortable she was, and how strange it felt to be sitting in Dillon's two-seater car, with all its small personal betrayals of him: today's newspaper and a map of the city on the floor under her feet; three pennies, a quarter and two nickels, a package of breath mints, and a restaurant check stub in the caddy at her elbow; his keychain—a brass oval with the initials DEJ on it—catching the light in minute flashes. She wondered what the E stood for. . . .

She tried hard not to think about the kiss, that incredible embrace . . . and, of course, in trying not to, she thought about it all the more. She'd never been so conscious of her body. She was conscious of every breath she took, every heartbeat. The sound of a swallow seemed shocking.

She felt so confused. She thought about the kiss, and the way he'd withdrawn from her afterward, just when she'd wanted so badly for him to kiss her again. Maybe, she thought, to him it had been no big deal. Maybe she was making too much of it. She wanted to ask him what was happening inside *him*, what the kiss had meant to him, and where things were going to go from here. But she didn't. Whatever was happening between them, it seemed too precarious just then, too fragile to talk about.

"Oh," she said in sheer relief when a lifetime later they pulled up in front of her sister's driveway. "Richard's home."

Dillon turned off the motor. "You said you live with your sister?" His tone was neutral, even cautious.

She nodded. "Yes."

"That surprises me."

"What does?"

"That a woman as independent as you are doesn't have a place of her own."

Funny, Tannis thought; she'd never felt ashamed before of being thirty years old with nothing to show for her life but a string of college degrees.

"I have lived alone," she said with a shrug. She felt flat, depressed. "In New York and L.A. . . . Paris. For the moment, this arrangement suits everyone concerned. I needed a base from which to conduct my research, and my sister offered. Her husband is a pilot on international flights and has to be away a lot, so they were both happy to have someone to keep Lisa and Josh company. We're a close family," she added when he went on looking at her. "We don't demand a lot of each other, but we're there for each other when it counts. . . . Does that answer your question?"

He nodded, frowning. "Yeah, that one. I have another one." There was a pause. She heard him take a deep breath. And then, very casually, he asked, "Are you seeing anyone?"

Tannis listened to the ticking sounds of the cooling engine, then asked, "Seeing anyone?"

Dillon made an impatient gesture. "Yeah. You're not married, or living with anybody. Are you . . . seeing anybody special?" There was another pause that seemed to stretch on forever. "Because if you're not, I'd like to. See you, I mean."

Tannis noticed that her heart had begun to beat hard and fast, as if something momentous were about to happen. "See me?" she asked faintly. "As in . . . date?"

The soft sound he made may have been laughter or exasperation, she thought.

"I guess you could call it that. I know I'd like to see you again . . . in the daylight, without having to peel and scrub you first." He paused. She caught a glitter in his eyes before he shuttered them with his lashes and brought their focus to rest on her mouth. And then, he whispered, "Will you have dinner with me tomorrow night?"

Her pulse was so violent, it rocked her. She listened to it for a few moments, thinking about the fact that only a little while ago she'd been wondering what might be happening between Dillon and her, feeling depressed because it didn't seem as if anything would. And now that something definitely was happening, she felt a sense of panic, as if she'd climbed aboard a fast freight without asking first were it was going.

"Tough question?" Dillon brushed her cheek with the backs of his fingers. Her breath sighed between her lips. As she fought an urge to close her eyes, she saw the wry lift of his smile and felt again that unanticipated surge of tenderness and excitement.

"All right," she heard herself say. "I will."

His hand dropped to her neck and cradled it warmly. "Great. Shall I pick you up at . . . say, seven?"

"All right."

His fingertips moved, down . . . up . . . feathering lightly over the bumps of her spine. She shivered, and to disguise the fact that she did, grabbed awkwardly for the door handle.

Dillon released her abruptly and started the car. "See

you tomorrow, then." She nodded and opened the door. "Oh, and, Tannis . . ."

She paused to look back, catching his smile. Again she felt that starburst of warmth in her chest.

Nodding at the bundle she held in her arms, he said, "Wear civilian clothes, huh?"

"Tannis Winter . . ." Logan said with interest, looking at Dillon across the disaster of his desktop. "Good Lord, the bag lady?"

"Come on, Logan, help me out." Dillon dropped into a chair and regarded the chief of police with exasperation. "Where am I going to take her for dinner?"

"You could always wait and see what she's wearing," Logan suggested, and held up a hand to ward off Dillon's rejoinder. "Now, wait, I didn't mean it *that* way. Although, if you want to spend your time with a woman who chooses to go around looking like Tugboat Annie when you could have any woman in this town from your own age bracket on down—which is a considerable span, by the way—that's your business."

Dillon glowered at him. "What do you mean, a considerable span? I'm not even forty."

"Pushin' pretty hard," Logan drawled, but Dillon wasn't paying attention.

"She's no Tugboat Annie," he said moodily, propping his head on his hand. "You know," he added thoughtfully, trying to put into the words the insight that had come to him just last night, "I get the feeling she does that—the clothes, the makeup—to hide herself. You know what I mean?"

Logan got a cop look on his face. "Hide? From what?"

"Not what, *who*," Dillon said, making an impatient erasing motion in the air with his hand. He paused, then said tentatively, "Me. I think she's hiding from me."

"Now, why on earth would she do a thing like that?"

Dillon shrugged. "I don't know. But I kind of have the feeling sometimes that she's afraid of me. Maybe not just me, maybe all men, maybe of getting involved, period. Hell, I don't know. I simply know she's afraid of something. Kind of makes me wonder if something might have happened to shake her confidence. You know what I mean? Like maybe she's been burned."

Logan shook his head, looking pained. "What do you want to mess with this for? I gotta tell you, buddy, I haven't seen you this uptight about a woman since Cindy kicked you out. Man, here you are, a free spirit at a time when single women outnumber single men about thirty to one, and you're tying yourself up in knots over a chick with a problem? Listen, trust me—you don't need this."

Dillon gave him a baleful look. "Where should I take her, Logan?"

"How about the Union Rescue Mission?"

"Very funny."

Tannis spent the afternoon agonizing over what to wear. She bounced from her closet to her dresser to the washing machine and ironing board to Lisa's closet and dresser, while her sister followed her around, asking questions she couldn't answer.

"Well, where is he taking you?"

"I don't know."

"Why didn't you ask him?"

"I don't know, I just didn't."

"Why don't you call him now and ask him?"

Tannis merely looked at her.

"Listen, why are you so frazzled about this? In the fifteen years since Mom and Dad started letting you go out alone with guys, I figure you've been through this only . . . oh, maybe a couple thousand times, right? You're acting like a high school kid! No—you're acting like *I* would have if anybody had ever asked me out in high school. You always had confidence. I've never seen you like this. Is it him? Do you have some sort of special feelings for him, is that it?"

"No!" Tannis stated emphatically. "I barely know him." Sure. And so far she'd knocked him windless in a gutter, gotten him arrested, kicked him in the shins, clobbered him with her purse, and embarrassed him in front of the entire city council. And what had he done to her? He'd given her a job, had very probably saved her life, and . . . he'd kissed her.

"Hmm," Lisa said. "Then it's you, I guess. Tan, what's happened to your self-confidence?"

"I don't know." Tannis groaned. "What should I do with my hair? Do you think I should wear it up?"

Lisa sighed and went off to check on Joshua, leaving Tannis gazing dispiritedly at her reflection in the mirror.

Is it him . . . or me? What's happened to my confidence?

She stared harder at her reflected image, trying to determine what other people saw when they looked at her. She saw an oval face with a belligerent chin, a nondescript mouth, a medium-sized nose with a smattering of freckles, blue eyes with dark brown brows and lashes, and hair that could be called either light brown or dark blond. Nothing special.

The truth was, she'd simply never worried much about her appearance; she'd always felt good about herself just because she had so many friends and seemed to make them so effortlessly. People liked her, she thought, because she genuinely liked people, and looks had nothing to do with it. Girls liked her because she was a good friend, fun to be with, and easy to talk to. She'd always thought boys liked her for the same reasons. Most of the boys she'd dated had been really good friends, and until Dan, it never occurred to her that any of them might have wanted to be something more.

Until Dan. Right from the start he'd made it plain that he wanted more from her than friendship. Dan

was older, in college, and well on his way to a career.
He was a young man who knew where he was going
and what he wanted, and one of the things he'd wanted
was Tannis. And beyond that she knew now that he
had truly and deeply loved her.

Her feelings for him had confused her. Just looking
at him and having him look back at her made her feel
disconnected, fragmented, as if everything inside her
were shaking loose. She loved talking with him, being
with him, doing things for him. She knew he was
everything she could ever want in a man, and she'd
often pictured herself spending the rest of her life with
him.

Oh, she'd told herself, but it was too soon! She was
too young—barely seventeen, with another year of high
school ahead of her, and after that, college, and Europe, and acting school. . . . It wasn't fair, she used to
think in the depths of the despair only seventeen-year-
olds seemed equipped to survive. Why did she have to
meet Dan then, when there was still so much she
wanted to do!

So she'd tried to make a friend of Dan, hoping, she
supposed, to sort of . . . keep him in the periphery of
her life until she was ready to commit herself. Like
putting him in the deep freeze. Only Dan wasn't buying
that. He'd forced her, in his quiet way, to make choices,
and so she'd made the only one she could. Even now,
after everything, she knew she couldn't really have done
things differently. The timing had been wrong.

So she and Dan had gone their separate ways, and
she had felt a cold emptiness inside her, a bleak sense
of loss. But she didn't forget him, and whenever she
saw him, which she did periodically during visits home,
she'd known in her heart that the feelings were still
there—for both of them. And always in the back of her
mind was the hope that someday, when she was ready
to settle down, she'd find a way to bring him back to
her. . . .

She shivered suddenly, and blinking her image into focus, saw a face that was deathly pale, a mouth that looked blurred, and eyes that had darkened with re-membered pain. Hating the look, she determinedly ban-ished it, lifting her chin and setting her mouth in lines of self-derision.

All right, so she'd gotten her comeuppance. Big deal. And why was she all of a sudden thinking about Dan so much anyway? He was ancient history!

Maybe, a niggling little voice in the back of her mind suggested, you're thinking about him because some-body who definitely is *not* ancient history reminds you a lot of him. . . .

No! she said staunchly to herself, Dillon James wasn't anything at all like Dan. And the way she felt when she was around Dillon certainly wasn't anything at all like the way she'd felt with Dan.

Of course, it wasn't anything like the way she usually felt with an attractive, interesting man either. She liked men . . . but she wasn't sure she liked Dillon. She couldn't think of him as a friend because she felt so uncomfortable with him. She didn't feel safe. She was used to being in control, being the one who set the tone and tempo of the relationship, but with Dillon . . . oh, Lord, with Dillon . . . She closed her eyes, feeling again that terrifying sensation of falling, that giddy upward surge inside her chest when he kissed her. With Dillon she definitely wasn't the one in control.

That was it, she thought with relief; she just needed to get back in control. Opening her eyes, she was pleased to see a bit of sparkle back in them. So a man had invaded her comfort zone before she was ready, and it had knocked her a little off balance. She'd handled that kind of thing before. All she had to do was keep him off balance instead.

The eyes in the mirror narrowed thoughtfully. Now, she thought, as for tonight . . . He'd asked her to wear "civilian clothes," but that could mean almost anything. So far, except for her bag lady's clothes, he'd seen her wearing jeans and a sweater, and toting a motorcycle helmet. What was the last thing he might expect of her tonight?

In the mirror Tannis watched her lips curve into a Mona Lisa smile.

Dillon wished he'd worn a tie. That was a spontaneous gut reaction; he knew he looked perfectly okay in slacks, dress shirt, sweater-vest, and sport jacket—and his favorite maroon one, at that. It was just kind of a shock, he told himself. He wasn't sure what he'd expected, but it wasn't this.

She was wearing black, something slim and slinky that didn't hug her body, but rather caressed it, moving subtly over its curves in a way that made his hands itch to do likewise. It had long sleeves, a scooped neck, and a pencil-slim skirt with a deep slit in the back; and when he put his hand on her back to usher her ahead of him through the door, he discovered that there was another slit in the top part of the dress, in a location that raised tantalizing questions about the nature of her underwear. Her legs were long and graceful in sheer black nylons and high-heeled shoes with open toes. Her hair was twisted and coiled high on her head with a few tendrils lying casually on her neck . . . and again his fingers tingled with the impulse to do the same.

Her adornment was simple and stunning: thin gold hoops in her ears, and a scarf in the rich jewel tones of garnet, black, and gold loosely arranged around her shoulders. Her makeup was flawless, accenting the haughty arch of her brows and lending her mouth a lush and sultry pout. She was a temptress, as sleek and seductive as an otter, expensive as ermine, elegant as mink. . . .

And, Dillon realized as she smiled up at him from under a sweep of dark lashes, this was no more the "real" Tannis than the bag lady had been. Funny, he thought as the disappointment registered itself in his consciousness, after his talk with Logan, he'd been half expecting her to put on some sort of protective camouflage again. And that was just what she'd done.

The ambiguity of his feelings irritated and confused him. In the first place, he didn't know why the bag-lady disguise annoyed him so, or why he'd felt such a yearning to see her face again in its natural state, so fresh and animated, with all her fire and enthusiasm showing in her eyes. And her body, tanned and supple, slender and graceful . . . He'd imagined her—well, to be honest, he'd imagined her pretty much the way a man might be expected to imagine a beautiful woman—in his arms, in varied and exciting ways.

But he'd discovered yesterday—to his considerable shock—that his desire to see and touch her wasn't just a physical thing. If it had been, he sure wouldn't have any reason to be disappointed now, would he? Because here she was, looking like a million dollars, and everything about her—the dress, the hair, the way she moved, even the look in her eyes—seemed to whisper seductively, *Touch me . . .*

And yet he knew it wasn't real. She was like an actress, costumed and in character for the role of the glamorous sophisticate. And the warm, passionate woman who had stood in his office and spoken of homeless people with tears in her eyes was still buried somewhere beneath that lovely, brittle shell.

"Very nice," Dillon exclaimed, knowing she waited for his response. Her response was a husky chuckle that grated on his nerves like nails on slate. Setting his teeth, he said smoothly, "Shall we go?" and offered her his arm.

As he walked her down the driveway to his car, he felt pressure in his jaws and made a conscious effort to relax them. He had an idea the smile on his face might have given Tannis pause if she'd happened to look up just then.

He was thinking about the way he'd peeled her mask from her once before—her physical mask, at least. Remembering the way he'd felt, kissing her, and her response to him, and the way it had seemed to compound and escalate so quickly. He remembered the way he'd had to clamp down on his own responses before they could escape his control.

He was wondering how long it would take him to strip this disguise away, and what might happen when he did.

The restaurant on the top floor of the Clifton Hotel was probably the closest thing to elegant dining Los Padres had to offer. The service was gracious, the decor heavy on natural wood, leather, brass, and candlelight, the food so-so, and the view magnificent, contrasting the milky rhinestone glitter of the Los Angeles basin on the north and west with the desert's brooding purple vastnesses and star-studded indigo sky.

Dillon hadn't made reservations, so they had drinks in the lounge by a gas log fire while they waited for a table. He ordered a club soda for himself and a margarita for Tannis.

There was a small dance floor and a fairly decent band. Dillon watched the firelight play over the back of Tannis's neck and across the curve of her cheek as she watched the dancers and the band. He watched the way she smiled and moved in response to the music, and after a while asked her if she'd like to dance. He knew by the quick way she turned and smiled at him, and the way the firelight flickered in her eyes, that she'd been hoping he'd ask.

It wasn't slow dancing, but Dillon didn't mind; that would come for them, too, he knew, in its own good time. Meanwhile, he liked watching her move to the heavy rock beat. He liked the way she danced, with him, even though they weren't touching, maintaining contact with her eyes. And through that contact Dillon felt a surge of exultation; for although Tannis might be dampening her natural enthusiasm and inhibiting her body movements to suit the role she'd chosen, she couldn't hide the flush of excitement in her cheeks or the sparkle of pure enjoyment in her eyes.

"That was fun," she said sedately when they left the dance floor.

Dillon just chuckled. The band was taking a break, and a piano player was getting ready to entertain the dinner crowd. Since there wasn't anything Dillon liked better than listening to a mellow piano, he ordered another club soda for himself and another margarita for Tannis and found a table nearby.

When the cocktail waitress had gone away, Tannis looked at Dillon and said, "You don't drink."

"No," he said, and shifted so that he could watch the piano player. He was deceptive, that piano player— reminded Dillon of his high school geometry teacher. But he sure did have a knack for evoking moods and memories. . . .

"Do you . . . have a problem with it?"

He glanced at her. She was frowning, playing with the salt crystals on the rim of her glass, licking them delicately from the tip of her index finger.

"I did once," he said, looking away again. "A long time ago. I'd rather not find out if I still do." The piano player's eyes met Dillon's across the top of the baby grand. Almost imperceptibly he nodded. *He knows,* Dillon thought, *he's been there too.*

He looked at Tannis and caught her studying him with an intent and thoughtful look. He knew what she was trying to do. She was trying to turn the tables on him with her personal questions, trying to crack him while she stayed safe and inviolate inside her elegant facade. But he had no intention of letting her succeed.

"What do you want to hear?" the piano man asked softly.

"How about . . . 'As Time Goes By'?" Dillon said without taking his eyes from Tannis's. He heard the soft hiss of an indrawn breath.

"You got it," the piano player said.

Dillon grinned and started to hum along with the melody of that most evocative of all saloon songs. After a moment, still holding fast to Tannis's luminous, transparent gaze, he began, very softly, to sing.

Eight

A kiss is still a kiss. . . .

The words stirred sensory memories in Tannis as they wafted across her. Her gaze drifted unbidden to Dillon's mouth and rested there, its focus narrowing until she could see nothing else at all. The room around her became warm and still.

You must remember this. . . . Oh, she did remember, not just with her mind but with all her senses. As she watched Dillon's mouth form the words of the song, she felt the movement of his lips on her own, inhaled the warm cinnamon scent of his breath, and tasted his essence on her tongue. Her body grew heavy and languid; she fought valiantly against the compulsion to close her eyes.

A sigh is just—

"James, party of two?"

Relief washed over her, shocking as a cold shower. She jerked her gaze to the hostess, feeling obscurely guilty and at the same time disoriented, as if she'd awakened abruptly in a strange place.

Control, she thought desperately as she got up to follow the smiling hostess. She had to maintain control. And she couldn't do that if she let herself think about that kiss, and the way his hands felt on her body. She mustn't think about those things at all.

For a while the procedures of being seated, perusing menus, making decisions, and ordering provided a welcome distraction. Finally, though, inevitably, the moment came when she and Dillon were left to confront each other across a small, intimate puddle of candlelight.

"So," Tannis said brightly in the silent wake of the departing waiter, "you said you used to be a cop?"

Dillon nodded, watching her through half-veiled eyes as he unhurriedly lifted his soda glass and drank. "That's what I said." His mouth curved, somewhat sardonically, she thought. "It was a long time ago."

"What made you decide to leave law enforcement?" A certain wariness in his attitude awakened her curiosity, and she forgot that she was only making conversation. She found she really did want to know the answer, along with many other things about Dillon James.

His gaze lowered, following the glass as he placed it carefully on the tablecloth. He shrugged. "Why does anyone change jobs? I just decided it wasn't what I wanted to do."

Unsatisfied, she persisted, "So you went into politics instead?"

He looked up at her in surprise. "Politics? Furthest thing from my mind, actually. No, I went into law. Criminal law. Only I couldn't decide what side of the fence I wanted to be on, so while I was trying to make up my mind, a friend of mine talked me into entering the city council race." His smile was both charming and dismissive. "Surprised the heck out of me when I won. Now then, you told me you've lived in Paris. I'd like to hear about that. . . ."

Tannis didn't mind having the conversation turned back to her. Regaling friends with lighthearted tales of her adventures—and misadventures—was one of the things she did best. She knew she was a gifted storyteller—animated and droll and often downright hilarious. It was a rare family gathering that she didn't have her parents looking dismayed and her brothers and Lisa all but rolling on the floor with laughter. And Dillon was a good listener, a responsive and appreciative audience. He seemed to relax; his full smile appeared often, and his laughter held genuine enjoyment.

They'd finished eating by the time she got around to New York, and her acting school and off-Broadway experience.

When she mentioned the acting, Dillon smiled and nodded, as if to himself. When Tannis said, "What?" he just shook his head and asked, "What made you give it up?"

"Acting?" She smiled and put on her bag lady's cracked and ruined voice. "I'm not sure I did give it up."

While Dillon was chuckling over that, she picked up his soda glass and toyed with it, mimicking his earlier gesture. As she placed the glass back on the table, she dropped her voice an octave and intoned, "Why does anybody change jobs? I just decided it wasn't what I wanted to do. . . ."

Dillon's laughter caused heads to turn their way. A small eruption of warmth filled Tannis's chest. She felt the warmth spread to her cheeks before she identified it as pleasure.

"I'll always love acting," she said softly. The twinkle in Dillon's eyes pricked her skin like the cold fire of Fourth of July sparklers.

"Cold?" he asked as she absently rubbed at the goose bumps on her arms.

"No," she said truthfully, "it's just . . . when I get emotional I get the shivers."

"I'll remember that." His chuckle was low and intimate; it triggered warning Klaxons in Tannis's head, and she shook it, like someone coming out of a daze.

Control . . . "Um," she said distractedly, "well, let's see, where was I?"

"Acting," Dillon prompted, looking amused.

"Yes." Tannis carefully cleared her throat. "I've always been a ham, I guess . . . loved to dress up, mimic people. That will never change. But while I was learning to observe people, to understand what makes them tick so I could interpret them as an actor, I found out I was more interested in the people than I was in the acting. Acting is fun, and seems to come naturally to me, but people fascinate me. So—" She lifted her shoulders as if to say, there you have it—"I've been studying them ever since."

"And in the meantime," Dillon said quietly, "you've never married."

"No." Her heart gave a little kick and picked up its pace. Darn him, somehow he'd managed to sneak up on her again. She had to be more alert.

"Why not?"

Steeling herself, she met his eyes and held steady under their regard. "That's a pretty personal question," she said evenly.

His voice became quieter still. "Tannis, don't you think it's time for personal questions?"

The candlelight seemed to waver. She turned her face to the dark glass and looked past the gold-tones reflected there to the big city brightness beyond. "Never met anyone I wanted to marry, I guess." She gave him the stock answer in a light, brittle voice.

"Never?"

There was a touch of militance in the look she turned back to him. "Look, marriage, kids, the little house in suburbia, the white picket fence—that stuff's not for me. I've got too many things I want to do—exciting things. *Important* things. It would take somebody pretty extraordinary to make me give all that up."

Dillon's eyebrows rose. "Why should you give it up? Haven't you heard? These are the eighties, you can have it all!"

"Yeah, sure, in theory maybe. But it's been my observation that once you've committed to those vows, the picket fence isn't far behind."

"Are you sure it's the picket fence you're afraid of," Dillon asked softly, "and not the commitment it stands for?"

There was a pause, filled with the tinkle of silver and crystal, soft ripples of conversation, and the sound of the piano playing a tune from Rodgers and Hammerstein whose title Tannis couldn't recall. And then she snapped, "What about you?" lifting the question out of the silence like a defensive parry. She glanced pointedly at the heavy signet ring on his left hand. "You're not married either."

His lashes dropped like shutters across his eyes. "I was once," he said in a neutral voice. "A long time ago."

"Divorced?"

He nodded.

A long time ago . . . It occurred to Tannis that a lot of things had happened to Dillon "a long time ago." She wondered what connection there might be between a failed marriage, a booze problem, and being a vice cop in downtown L.A. . . .

"Any children?"

"No." He reached for the check tray and became very busy sorting out his change. "No children." He handed her a candy mint. "Shall we go?"

"Speaking of children," he said casually as he came around to help her out of her chair, "why haven't you told anyone about the kids in that vacant lot?"

Dillon had known he would her ask her about the children at some point—he just hadn't known he was going to do it right then. Her response made him feel half triumphant, half ashamed. She froze and threw him a quick guilty look that was replaced by one of momentary panic, as if, he thought, she'd almost swallowed her after-dinner mint.

"How . . .." she began, then stopped.

She would have sunk back into her chair, but Dillon inserted a hand under her elbow and firmly raised her to her feet. "It looks like the band is coming back," he said smoothly. "Shall we have our coffee in the lounge?"

On their way through the dining room he snagged a passing cocktail waitress and put in his request for coffee.

When he caught up with Tannis in the darkened lounge, she said furiously, "I want to know how you found out about—"

At that moment the band launched loudly into its late-evening set with a current rock hit, effectively putting an end to conversation. Dillon lowered his head until his lips brushed the tendrils of hair near her ear and said loudly, " Sorry—can't hear a word you're saying. Guess we might as well dance."

Managing to place his hand squarely over the slit in the back of the bodice of her dress, he steered her deftly toward the dance floor. A little tremor rippled beneath his hand. He wondered whether it was caused by anger or by fear.

She danced differently now—a little clumsily, he thought, steadfastly refusing to look at him—but he enjoyed watching her all the same. Anger and exercise— and maybe the margaritas—had touched her cheeks with color and made her eyes sparkle as if she'd just come in from a romp in the snow. A few more tendrils of hair came loose to waft gently around her face or cling damply to her temples and the nape of her neck. The scarf around her shoulders got in her way, and she snatched it off with an impatient gesture that reminded Dillon of a flamenco dancer. She looked exotic and passionate . . . and he was stirred by the sight of her, more than he'd been stirred in a very long time.

The song ended. Tannis turned to leave the floor, but the band, with only the briefest of pauses, slipped easily into the moody rhythms of a pop standard. Dillon caught her arm at the elbow. She hesitated, then lifted her chin and threw him a look of challenge over her shoulder. He felt his chest expand with a strange excitement as he pulled her into his arms.

She moved easily but resisted closeness, maintaining space between their bodies as she tipped her head back and looked straight into his eyes. "You followed me, didn't you?" Her voice was accusing, and as cold as her last name. "That's how you managed to be there to—"

"Save your life?" Dillon said pleasantly.

Her eyes faltered; her breath sighed through parted lips. In that moment of uncertainty he drew her close and experienced the remainder of her exhalation as a kind of melting of her body against his own. His hand sought the bare skin between her shoulder blades; his fingertips moved up and down in the gentle indentation of her spine, just barely brushing the fine hairs that gave her skin the texture of velvet.

"I knew it!" she whispered furiously, her breath warm on his collar. "Once a cop, always a cop!" But he felt the betraying tremors inside her. And when he moved his hand farther down and splayed his fingers over the small of her back, pressing to bring her lower body into exquisite contact with his, he heard the sharp catch in her breathing.

Sorry now that he'd brought the coldness of the street between them, he led her in simple, uncomplicated movements, wanting her to think of nothing but the way his thighs slid against hers as they swayed together, and the way their heartbeats merged in a duet of syncopated rhythms. He wanted her to be deaf to the music; he wanted her to be dizzy, but not from the dancing. He wanted her to lose all sense of time and space while her nerve endings awakened to the newness of *his* touch.

He hooked her hand around his neck, freeing his own to gently massage her upper back. His fingertips teased the silky ribbons of her hair and burrowed under them to trace the curve of her skull, kneading the vulnerable cords and hollows until her neck lost rigidity and her head tipped forward, bringing her moisture-beaded brow to rest against his lips. He moved his open mouth back and forth across her forehead, then blew softly on her temple . . . and felt the hand on the back of his neck tremble.

Under his hand her neck muscles felt liquid and malleable. It took so little pressure to tilt her head so that her face was slowly lifted to his. His mouth slid downward, tenderly brushing an eyebrow, a quivering eyelid, mink-soft lashes, and a dewy cheek. When he came to her lips and found them parted, he paused there, barely touching her, while her warm breath bathed his lips with the scent of mint.

He heard a tiny, desperate sound. Her muscles jerked suddenly. The hands on his neck tightened, clutched at his shoulders, then flattened against his chest. Her eyes opened wide; he had one gut-wrenching glimpse into them before she broke from his arms. What he saw there shocked him so badly, he let her go.

Panic—sheer panic. He'd seen that look in her eyes once before, when he'd accosted her in his wino's rags. He hadn't liked it much then. Right now he felt as if she'd punched him in the stomach.

It was several minutes before he could go after her. He had to pay for the coffee he'd ordered and retrieve the coat she'd forgotten. He stuck his head in the ladies' room door, to the profound dismay of its current occupants, on the off chance she'd sought a temporary refuge there, then rode the elevator to the main lobby in an agony of frustration, knowing he was almost certainly too late to catch her.

In the lobby he described Tannis to both the desk clerk and the doorman, but neither had seen her go by. Finally, figuring she'd somehow slipped past them unseen, he took the elevator to the parking garage. If she was out there, it had to be on foot, and he stood a better chance of finding her in his car.

She was waiting for him, leaning against the front fender of his car, idly pulling her scarf back and forth through her fingers.

"I figured you'd end up here eventually," she said in a froggy voice.

Dillon stopped a few yards away, put his hands in his pockets, and looked at her.

"I'm sorry. I shouldn't have run out on you like that. It was childish." The last word ended with a tight, choking sound.

Knowing she was crying but not quite ready to forgive her for the shock she'd dealt him, Dillon said harshly, "Why did you?"

She shrugged, opened her mouth and closed it again, gave the scarf a helpless little wave, and abruptly turned her back to him. Now that his heart rate had slowed and his breath no longer burned his chest, Dillon moved close to her. "Want to talk about it?" he asked after clearing his throat of lingering traces of hoarseness.

When she only shook her head, he reached out to her, fitting his palms to her shoulders and kneading in a gentle circular motion. "Tannis . . ."

"No . . . please! Don't—" It was a cry that lacerated his heart. "Don't touch me like . . . that!"

"Like this?" he said huskily and, turning her, took her face between his hands and held it as if it were a priceless treasure. As he raised her face to the light, he saw that her eyes were so tightly closed there were stress lines in the center of her forehead, like a watermark on satin, and that her mouth had a soft, blurred look. A tiny tear quivered at its corner. He brushed it away with his thumb just before he lowered his head and covered her mouth with his.

He kissed her with a tenderness he hadn't known he was capable of; a sweet, aching tenderness that somehow rendered him as fragile as she. When her mouth trembled under his, he felt the same trembling within himself; and when she whimpered, the cry pierced him to the depths of his soul.

She tried to pull away from him, but this time he was ready for her. "Tannis," he said, his voice hoarse and gritty, "what is it? What's *wrong*?"

Since he wouldn't let her run away, she had to shield her naked emotions from him by covering her face with her hands. "I don't . . ." She drew in a sobbing breath. "I don't want to feel like this. I didn't . . . ever want to feel like this again!"

"Feel like . . ." he began, bewildered. And then, as understanding came to him, he gently pulled her hands away. Her eyes stared up at him through a curtain of tears. "Why not?" he asked softly, brushing her lips with his thumb.

Fueled only by a shallow, quivering breath, her voice emerged precariously. "It hurts . . . too much!" And then her mouth and eyes clamped shut once more.

"Oh, God." Dillon drew her close, cradling her head against his chest. There was something almost reflexive about the way he folded himself around her, as if he were protecting both her and his own vulnerable parts.

And while he held her that way, he wondered how it could have happened, how he could have left himself open to such an emotional onslaught. After ten years of exposure to the whole rotten range of human suffering, how could something like this strike so deeply at the strongholds of his heart?

"Tannis," he said as soon as he could speak again, "loving isn't supposed to hurt. Who's hurt you, baby?" When she didn't answer, he held her awhile longer and tried again. "Did someone hurt you?" She nodded. "Do you want to talk about it?" She shook her head emphatically. After a moment Dillon cleared his throat and said slowly, "I think you have to, babe. I think you're long overdue."

Taking her by the arms, he separated himself from

her just far enough so that he could look at her. "You can trust me, you know," he said. "I'd never hurt you like that. The last thing I'd ever want to do is hurt you." And as he listened to the echoes of his voice, it stunned him to realize that he meant every word.

"Talk to me," he pleaded through emotion-tensed jaws. "Talk to me."

It seemed like a long time before he felt her muscles relax and heard her soft sigh of capitulation. "It's no big deal," she said, swiping angrily at her eyes. "It's silly."

"Tell me anyway." When she shivered, he pulled her coat around her shoulders.

"I'm not sure I can."

"Of course you can," Dillon said grimly. "You start by telling me his name."

In the anonymous darkness of Dillon's car, with the motor running and the heater going full blast, Tannis talked about Dan. Dillon sat facing forward, and so did she; it was easier that way, like being in a confessional. She told him the easy stuff first, about how it had been in high school, and about meeting Dan, and all the little traumas and tragedies that came with being seventeen and in love before your time. It was like talking about something that had happened to somebody else, or like telling the plot of a movie she'd seen.

It was harder to tell him about the years after that. She wasn't sure why she did. There was just something about the way he sat so quietly, a comforting presence in the darkness, not demanding or judging, simply . . . listening. She kept thinking about his words: *You can trust me. I'll never hurt you.* She didn't know why she believed him, but she did.

"I don't know if you can understand this," she said after a little silence, turning to look at him for the first time. He waited silently for her to go on, and after a moment she did. "The thing about virginity"—she felt his little start of surprise—"is that the longer you keep it, the harder it is to let go of it. At least that's the way it was with me. I saw so many of my friends, and the way they were hurt by it—by sex, I mean—the regrets they had, the loss of self-esteem. And I was determined that wasn't going to happen to me. Making love was going to be something *special*, and it wasn't going to happen until *I* was ready. That's why I didn't make love with Dan, I think. Even though I loved him, I just knew I wasn't ready for that kind of relationship, you know?"

She flicked Dillon a glance, half fearfully, and found that he had turned and was looking at her now. Taking a quick, sharp breath, she faced forward again and went on. "Anyway, if you get past the age of rebellion and experimentation and you're still a virgin, it seems like—I don't know—something you have to make excuses for. Guys don't want to deal with an inexperienced innocent, I guess. And then there was the way I felt about it. I still wanted the first time to be . . . special. I still wanted to be in love. Of course"—she gave a high little laugh—"the way I am, I fall in love every other week. But somehow, whether it was because of the way I still felt about Dan, or because there was so much I wanted to do with my life, nothing ever seemed to develop into a real relationship. Either I'd meet somebody else absolutely fascinating—for a little while—and off I'd go, or he'd get tired of being held at arm's length while I tried to make up my mind to go to bed with him. I could have, so many times. But after waiting so long—"

"Tannis," Dillon said, his voice sounding rusty, "if you're trying to apologize for still being a virgin, don't."

"But I'm not one," she said flatly. "Not anymore."

"I see," he said, and waited. Finally, he gently prompted her. "What happened, babe?"

She swallowed. "I met Dan again." She heard the sigh of an exhalation. Glancing at Dillon, she saw that he'd put a hand over the bottom part of his face. She smiled thinly. "Yeah, I know. It was about a year ago. I ran into him at a seminar in San Diego, of all things. We started talking about old times, and wound up having dinner together. I had a little bit too much to drink, I guess—I was probably nervous, seeing him again after so long. We danced. I don't remember too much about what happened, but eventually we, um . . . ended up in my room together."

She stopped. Dillon didn't say anything. After a moment she coughed carefully and went on. "It was . . . everything I'd hoped it might be. The feelings were still there—for me. And I thought they were for him too. I thought—"

"It's okay," Dillon said, touching her hand.

"He didn't—" She took a deep breath, and this time, by making her voice low and breathy, she was able to slip it past the lump that lurked in her throat. "He didn't actually tell me he'd made love to me only as a sort of . . . I don't know, revenge for my rejection of him all those years ago. He wasn't that brutal. Just . . . cold. And final. He told me it had been a mistake. He was in love with someone—about to be married, in fact—and that he took full responsibility for what had happened between us, that both of us had had too much to drink and had gotten carried away with memories of old times. Well, you can imagine the rest. In short—Hey, it's been nice seeing you again, Tan. So long. . . ."

She scrunched down in her seat, brushing angrily at her eyes. "*Damn.* It was such a shabby little scene, you know? I'll bet it's happened to millions of other women—men, too, probably. I don't know why I'm making such a fuss about it. But—darn it." She put her hand over her eyes.

"But it hurts," Dillon said softly.

"Yes. It did hurt. At the time I thought I was going to die. First it was so wonderful . . . I'd never felt that way before. And then—"

Dillon put the car in gear so abruptly it startled her. She sniffed and sat up straight. "Where are we going?"

"I don't know." She caught the flash of his lopsided grin. "I just needed to do something, know what I mean?"

"Yes," she said, instantly contrite. "Hey, I'm sorry. I didn't mean to lay all this—"

"Don't be sorry. I asked you to, remember?" He threw her a rueful glance. "Any suggestions? We never did have our coffee?"

"Well," she said, clearing her throat, "would you like to go to my place? We'd have to stop somewhere and get the coffee though."

"That would be fine. I'd like to meet your sister."

Warmed by the sound of his voice, Tannis laughed, a little uncertainly, a lot relieved, like someone who has emerged from a dreaded ordeal unscathed. "I didn't say my sister's place. I said *mine*. It's not far from here."

He looked wary but intrigued. "Okay."

Tannis touched his hand. In a voice still hoarse with emotion, she said, "Dillon? Thanks . . . you're an unexpected friend."

His head swiveled toward her slowly. The look he gave her this time was long and enigmatic. And then, without saying anything, in a gesture that hinted of possession and passion and loving restraint, he caught her hand and carried it to his thigh. He held it there while he drove, pressed tightly against his firm, resilient muscles. Something about the set of his profile and the rigidity of his silence made Tannis wonder if she'd said something to hurt him.

"I'd planned to bring you here eventually," Tannis said. As she moved away from him across the rooftop, a cold wind lifted the tendrils of hair from her neck and found its way inside her coat. She drew it more tightly around herself and shivered, then laughed and held up the pair of high-heeled shoes that dangled from her hand. "I just didn't expect it to be tonight. These weren't exactly meant for climbing fire escapes! Brrr! It really feels like winter tonight, doesn't it? But then, it's always windy up here. That's why nobody sleeps up here in the wintertime. Right now I have it pretty much to myself most of the time. In the summer, though, the street people like to come up here in the evenings—the regulars, anyway, the ones who know—"

"—Every lock that ain't locked when no one's around," Dillon quoted dryly.

He knew that she was chattering to fill up the silence, but he didn't feel like making it any easier for her. Damn her, so she thought she had him all tucked away into that safe little slot marked "friend," did she? A sense of frustration and futility chilled him more than the wind, and made him curl his hands into fists and thrust them deep in his pockets. He'd never known anyone so fearful of intimacy, nor anyone with so many ways of warding it off! He'd already learned that Tannis's disguises were clever and varied; now he was discovering the most impregnable of all her defenses.

Friendship. The value of friendship . . . don't want anything to spoil our friendship . . . How noble and sincere it all sounded. But it merely threw up walls around her. And it handcuffed him completely. The control was in her hands; she'd given him a set of rules, and any attempt on his part to break them would be taken as a violation of the trust and sanctity of the *friendship.*

And the funny thing was, she was a psychologist. He was almost certain that if he asked her, she'd tell him she firmly believed that a loving, intimate relationship should be based on a solid friendship. He didn't think she had any idea she was using friendship as a way to avoid intimacy. As a child she'd felt secure in friendships, and she'd brought that security with her into adulthood. It had worked for her so well . . . with one exception.

It hadn't worked for her when she'd needed it most. The one time she'd opened herself up to intimacy, she'd ended up getting clobbered. Bleakly Dillon wondered whether she'd ever trust enough to let her guard down again.

Tannis's laughter was a light, brittle sound that set his teeth on edge. "Yes," she said, "the street people do seem to know all the city's nooks and crannies, the ones that have been around awhile anyway." Hugging her coat around her, she walked slowly to the waist-high wall that bordered the edge of the roof and stood there, gazing out over the city. "Do you know what the homeless people see from up here?" Her voice drifted back to him on the bitter wind. "Come here. . . .

"Out there," Tannis said when he joined her. She indicated the suburban sprawl with a movement of her head. "On warm summer nights you can stand up here and hear voices of people in their backyards—children splashing in their swimming pools, husbands and wives bickering about whose turn it is to take out the garbage. You can smell food cooking on outdoor barbecues.

"And some street people don't mind being up here instead of down there. They wouldn't live in one of those houses even if you gave it to them free of charge. Sometimes I think . . . it must seem to them like living in a cage."

And you feel an affinity for them, Dillon thought as he watched stray curls blow around her face and neck. He understood her better now, but his understanding brought him no comfort. His jaws felt tight as he asked her, "What about the ones who don't prefer being up here—or out there, on the streets. Or in abandoned cars in vacant lots."

"The children, you mean." She turned to face him, her chin rose defensively.

"Yes. The children. Tannis, why didn't you tell me

about them? Why haven't you done anything about them?"

"I have done something! I take them food—"

"You know what I mean! We can't help everybody out there, but for God's sake, a whole family of *children*? There are organizations. I could have—"

"That's what *you* think! There aren't any organizations to help illegals. Except to help them out of the country!" She was breathing hard, her anger flaring quick and hot.

Dillon rubbed a hand over his face and let his breath out slowly. "Illegals." He swore softly. "Is that what they are?"

Just as quickly as it had erupted, her anger died, leaving her oddly defenseless. "I think so," she whispered. "I think they must be."

"You *think*? Haven't you talked to them?"

"Well, yes and no. My Spanish isn't very good. But I think they must be illegals. They're all so frightened."

"Where's the father?"

Tannis shrugged. "I don't know that either, but whenever I ask, they seem even more afraid. I think maybe they got separated at the border or something. Dillon, what if he's looking for them? How will he ever find them?"

"Tannis," he said grimly, taking her arms, "you've got to take me there. My Spanish is very good. Please, let me talk to them." Sensing her wariness, he moved his hands up and down on the sleeves of her coat, acknowledging some irony as he added, "As . . . a friend?"

"Oh, Dillon, I'm sorry." Contrite, she reached impulsively to touch him. Her hands felt warm on his windchilled jaws. "I should have trusted you. You've been so wonderful. I know you're my friend. I guess if I can trust anybody, it's you."

"Thanks," Dillon said sardonically, gently but firmly pulling her hands away from his face. There were some things his flayed emotions weren't up to dealing with right at that moment, and her touch was at the top of the list. "First thing tomorrow morning we both pay a visit to that vacant lot. But right now I'd like to get off this roof before I freeze to death." He looked down at her hands and, aching with longing, enfolded them in both of his for one brief moment. "Your hands are so warm," he said, feeling choked. "Aren't you cold?"

"Oh, not really." Her tone was blithe and airy as she stepped ahead of him onto the fire escape. "I don't mind the cold. I guess I must be a true winter's child. . . ."

As he followed her down those iron stairs, as he listened to her chatter away beside him in the car, and finally, as he said a chaste and "friendly" good night to her at her sister's door, Dillon was thinking that loving a winter's child might turn out to be a bleak and lonely business.

Nine

Tannis sat on the rusted, dirty fender of a stripped-down car body, peeling an orange while a dark-haired child leaned against her leg and watched the movements of her hands with great, famished eyes. Tannis's eyes were on Dillon, who was standing a few yards away talking to the child's mother in earnest, staccato Spanish.

Dillon. His friendship seemed like a miracle to her. Just yesterday she'd felt uncertain and off balance about her feelings for him; today she felt secure and once again in control. And more. For the first time in years she could think of Dan without pain. She was really and truly free of him, and she knew she had Dillon to thank for it.

He really is a special person, she thought, watching him as he focused his attention on the homeless woman, bending his head in order to hear every word she spoke, touching her arm in a gesture of reassurance. The sight of him filled Tannis with a strange effervescence, a kind of light but expanding pressure that made her straighten her body and square her shoulders in order to make room for it. And when it overflowed, she had to break into a smile.

Her smile brought a giggle of response from the child at her knees. "There you go, sweetheart," she murmured, handing over the peeled orange. The child took it with a whispered, "*Gracias*," and scurried off to join her brothers and sisters.

Tannis wiped her sticky hands on her thighs and thought as she did so that one of the nicest things about friends was that you didn't have to worry about impressing them. She felt completely comfortable with Dillon now, wearing her favorite knocking-around clothes—her oldest, softest jeans, Reeboks, and a sweatshirt from London's Hard Rock Cafe—no makeup at all, not even lipstick, and her hair in its usual multi-layered disarray. What a contrast, she thought in amusement, between the woman who'd answered Dillon's knock this morning and the one he'd dined and danced with last night! And the nice thing was, she knew from his smile and the warmth in his eyes that he hadn't been disappointed with the way she looked, that he'd simply been glad to see her.

She was a little less certain about her own reaction upon opening her sister's front door to find Dillon standing there looking lean and masculine, but with that just-showered, freshly shaved look that was somehow so appealing. He was wearing jeans as worn and faded as hers, a cream-colored cable knit sweater, and a brown bomber jacket that looked lived-in enough to have been a favorite since long before they'd become fashionable. He'd smelled of soap and clean clothes and old leather, and she'd felt a most unfriendlike urge to throw her arms around him and breathe in the scent of him, and lay her cheek against his smooth, moist skin and press her lips against the warm, strong column of his neck.

Thinking about it now as she watched him come toward her, putting his sunglasses on, she felt that lurch in her chest and stomach, that sensation of falling. . . .

"Come on, let's go." He looked grim. Though his eyes were hidden behind the glasses, his jaw was rigid, his mouth a thin, angry line.

As she slid down off the fender, Tannis looked past him to where the woman stood holding her youngest child in her arms. She clung to the baby as if she feared he was about to be snatched from her. Her stoic demeanor had given way to a haunted, hopeless look.

Tannis questioned the wisdom of coming here without her bag-lady clothes. Although the children had excitedly clustered around the younger, well-groomed "Win," their mother hadn't been so accepting. The glimmer of suspicion burned in her eyes like a warning light.

"Is anything wrong?" Tannis asked, uncertainly brushing at the seat of her pants.

Dillon just shook his head and took her elbow in a grip hard enough to make her wince. He muttered a distracted, "Sorry," as he released her, and used the hand, instead, to rake at his hair.

Tannis touched him reassuringly as she called goodbye to the children. As she walked with him to his car, she kept stealing sideways glances at him, seeking her own reassurance. But though she could see a muscle working rhythmically in his jaw, and knew he must be aware of her concern, he didn't look at her once.

He opened the door for her, then got into his own side and started the engine. He pulled away from the curb slowly and drove in silence with one hand covering the lower half of his face. All his movements were restrained, almost frighteningly controlled. The silence thickened and became a wall around him while Tannis sat helplessly wondering how in the world she was ever going to find a way to penetrate it.

They were driving through a shabby but quiet residential neighborhood, when Dillon suddenly whipped the car over to the curb and jerked to a stop. For a few moments they both sat still, Tannis blinking dazedly,

Dillon gripping the steering wheel and staring straight ahead. And then he leaned forward and dropped his forehead onto his hands.

Tannis slowly loosened the fingers that had wrapped themselves reflexively around the door handle. It frightened her to see Dillon like this. Their friendship was too new. She didn't know what to do. She didn't know what was wrong. She wanted so badly to reach out to him, touch him, hold him—and for the first time in her life, she didn't seem to know how. She'd always been a compassionate person, a loyal and caring friend; she was a born communicator and a professional psychologist to boot—and she didn't have a clue what to say to Dillon now. It was a terrible feeling . . . a lonely feeling.

Now she understood how Dillon must have felt last night when she'd left him standing in the middle of a dance floor. She remembered the way his voice had sounded when he'd first spoken to her in the garage, as if he'd had to force it past shards of broken glass. She remembered his words. . . .

In the same desperate way she cried, "Dillon, what is it? What's *wrong*?"

After an eternity he drew an uneven breath and sat back, leaving Tannis so awash with relief she felt queasy.

"I'm sorry," he said. "I didn't think it could still affect me like that."

"What? You didn't think *what* could affect you?"

Dillon took off his sunglasses and turned to face her. "They aren't illegals. Tannis, she's afraid of her *husband*. She—the whole family, all of them—are in that damned junkyard because they're scared to death of him."

"Afraid . . . of her husband? You mean he's—"

Dillon nodded, a violent motion that was at once both confirming and rejecting. "Abusive. Yes." He took another of those great breaths and slowly let it out. "Apparently he's a citizen; she and the kids aren't. He managed to get permission for them to come here about a year ago, but I think he must have kept them pretty well isolated, because none of them speaks English, and the kids haven't been going to school. I guess he's always had a tendency to knock them around when he's been drinking. . . ." He stopped, coughed, and went on. "But she says that it got a lot worse after the baby was born. He accused her of being unfaithful to him. Even says the little one isn't his. He's beaten her—the mother—pretty badly on several occasions, and she's afraid he might try to harm the baby. I think what she's really afraid of is what would happen to the baby if . . . if she weren't around anymore to protect him."

"If he kills her, you mean. Or puts her in the hospital. Oh, God." Tannis sat still with her hand over her mouth. "But why didn't she go to the police? What about her own family?"

Dillon shook his head. His face looked drawn and tired. "She thought the police wouldn't believe her, that they'd either send her back to her husband, or that he'd find out somehow where she was. As for her family back in Mexico, they are of the belief that a wife's place is with her husband—to honor and obey until death do them part."

Tannis shivered. "But there are shelters . . . there's help for people like her."

"I told her that. Right now she's trying to decide whether or not she believes me. I told her we'd come back tomorrow."

"Oh, Dillon, I hate to think of them out there another night. It's getting colder. I think it's going to rain."

"Yeah, I know. Unfortunately she'd rather face the cold than her husband. *Damn.* If they'd just known where to go . . . who to call." He rubbed his eyes as if they hurt him, then he put his dark glasses back on and reached for the ignition key.

"Dillon . . ." Tannis put her hand on his, stopping

him. "You had an idea about this, didn't you? Even before you talked to her."

"Yeah." His voice sounded curiously hollow. "I had an idea. And as soon as I saw her, I knew. I knew the look. I'd seen it before."

"As a cop, you mean?"

"No. Not as a cop." He turned to look at her, and it was the derelict's face she saw . . . cold, bleak, dark. *The dark side* . . . Only now, instead of being afraid of that side of him, she wanted to put her arms around him and hold him tightly until the darkness went away.

He went on looking at her with anguish in his eyes, unable to say anything more. He didn't have to. Aching with compassion and understanding, Tannis looked back at him, and this time when he reached for the ignition key, she didn't stop him.

"Well," Dillon said, "here we are."

Tannis just nodded and went on staring absently at an overturned tricycle in the driveway.

Dillon didn't see the tricycle's owner anywhere; in fact, for a Sunday noon, the whole street seemed unnaturally deserted. Everyone was indoors having brunch, Dillon supposed, curled up by the fire, reading the funny papers. It was the right sort of day for it, with the clouds thickening and the wind turning blustery. Looked like a storm blowing in. About time, he thought, after the long warm, dry spell. He sighed inwardly. In some ways a good rain was more than welcome, but it sure was going to make things worse for the street people.

He shifted his focus to Tannis, guessing by the look on her face that she was thinking the same thing. Probably thinking about those kids in that vacant lot. Her profile had a particularly bleak look, which mirrored the way Dillon felt. But he knew he'd done all he could do for now. He could only wait for that poor woman to make up her mind to trust him.

Meanwhile, he didn't want to think about it anymore. He wanted—*damn*! He knew exactly what he wanted, but he couldn't let himself think about that either. He didn't dare allow himself to think about Tannis having brunch with him in front of his fireplace, laughing with him at the comics, making love in the warm glow of firelight. . . . *No.* He definitely couldn't think about that.

He wondered why she just kept sitting there, staring out the window. He wished she'd say good-bye and go—quickly. The longer she sat there, the more he hated the thought of her going. If she stayed much longer, he was going to lose control and reach for her, and that, he knew, would be disastrous. As afraid as she was of intimacy, if he made a move before she was ready, she'd panic again, and this time he might even lose her friendship. He couldn't risk it. He wanted her in his life, and if, for now, it had to be on her terms, so be it. He could be patient when he had to be.

But he wondered why she didn't get out of the car. The suspense was killing him.

And then he decided he really should see her to the door. Maybe, he thought resentfully, that was what she was waiting for—although it didn't seem to him like it ought to be required of a *friend*.

Feeling put upon and out of sorts, Dillon reached for the door handle and gave it a yank. "Well—" he began at precisely the same moment Tannis turned toward him and said, "Dillon—"

"What?" He waited, counting heartbeats.

"I don't . . ." She stopped herself. When she continued, her voice was barely audible. "I don't feel like going home."

Dillon's heartbeats grew louder. "What do you feel like doing?"

She shrugged. "I don't know. It's Sunday, and it's

cold and dismal, and after . . . it just seems . . . I thought, if you didn't have anything better to do, maybe we could have lunch?"

Dillon carefully cleared his throat and said, "All right with me. Did you have anyplace special in mind?"

"No," she said, "not really."

Through the thunder in his ears Dillon heard himself say, "Would you like to come out to my place?"

Why do people always think of deserts as flat? Why do California towns have city limits signs in the middle of nowhere?

Those were a couple of the things Tannis thought about on the way to Dillon's house on the farthest eastern outskirts of the city. She thought about them to keep from thinking about Dillon.

It was hard to tell what Dillon was thinking about. He drove as he so often did, with one hand covering the lower part of his face, and his brooding and strangely electric silence left a lot of room for speculation.

What must it have been like, the cataclysm that tore apart the earth and thrust whole sections of its crust toward the sky?

But the tortured and beautiful landscape and it's mute evidence of ancient upheavals made Tannis think about another kind of cataclysm, the kind that strikes the human heart—suddenly, devastatingly, and utterly without warning.

"This is it," Dillon announced unnecessarily as he pulled the car into a driveway that led to a garage on an upper level of the house. "I'll show you around later, if that's okay. Right now, I don't know about you, but I'm ready to eat something."

"Fine," Tannis said tightly.

Dillon's home was a surprise to her. Though they were only a few miles from downtown Los Padres, the desert here seemed remarkably unencroached upon, the houses custom-built and widely scattered. Some of them, including this one, blended with the landscape, became a part of a delicate tapestry of striated pink and purple hills, yellow sagebrush, and gray-green yuccas and joshua trees. Partly set into the side of a hill, the house reminded Tannis of an ancient pueblo, with its sand-colored walls, softened lines, and subtle angles. But there were unmistakably modern touches, too, like the walls of glass strategically placed so as to get the maximum benefit from the desert sun.

"Is it all solar heated?" she asked, spotting the panels on the south-facing roof.

Dillon nodded. "And cooled. I have a back-up natural gas system for water heating. Logan claims he uses one hundred percent solar to heat both his pool and the Jacuzzi, but I find that a little hard to believe."

"Logan?"

"Yeah . . . you met him the other day, remember? Chief of police. That's his place down there. He put in a pool because of his kids. I decided for the amount of use I'd get out of it, it wasn't worth the trouble, and besides, if I really want to swim, I can always use his. I do, however, have a Jacuzzi. It's, uh—" He coughed and, with an endearing awkwardness, pushed open the door and held it for her. "Well, here we are. Please excuse the mess. I haven't had much luck with housekeepers."

"Oh." Tannis sighed, for somehow he had brought the desert's beauty inside. Airy, vaulted ceilings, pale wood floors, Navaho rugs . . . sand, terra cotta, and touches of sky blue. "It's lovely."

"Thanks. Kitchen's in here." Half smiling, he waited for her reaction.

She didn't disappoint him. "Wow, what is this? Are you a gourmet cook?" The kitchen was a dream, tile and wood and hanging copper pots and every convenience imaginable.

Dillon's chuckle was sardonic. "Sure. I'm a wizard

with a microwave." With a grand flourish he threw open the door to a full-sized freezer. "What'll it be? Shrimp Cantonese? Chicken à l'orange. Eggplant Parmesan? Pepperoni pizza?"

"Good Lord," Tannis said faintly, gazing at the most incredible array of frozen foods she'd ever seen outside a supermarket.

"Take your pick. Unless *you* like to cook?"

She gave him a wary look. "Though I do get the urge now and then, if I had to cook, I'd hate it. I'll have the fish Florentine. And a blueberry muffin, please," she added politely.

Dillon couldn't decide between pasta primavera and chili with corn bread, so he took them both.

While they waited for the oven's beep, Dillon unwrapped the *Los Angeles Times* and sorted through it for the comics section.

They ate perched on stools before a counter of terracotta tile while a famous chef's fabulous gourmet dessert defrosted slowly in the microwave. Tannis didn't know what it was called, but it involved chocolate fudge cake and hot raspberry sauce.

"I can't believe I ate that," she groaned sometime later, licking the last of the sauce from her lips. "I can't believe *you* ate it—on top of pasta and chili and corn bread. How do you stay so thin?"

"Hmm." He stared at her so intently, she began to think she'd asked a very dumb—or very personal—question. Then he said, "Hold still." He reached out and drew his thumb across her upper lip, then popped it into his own mouth.

It was a gesture of such casual, spontaneous intimacy, it took her breath away.

"Come on," he said abruptly, taking her wrist and pulling her off her stool, "let's go walk off some calories. I'll show you my kingdom. . . ."

"It's *raining*!" she gasped as they stepped outside.

"So it is." Dillon squinted up at the sky, then down

at her. His eyes had an odd brightness. "Cold?" Light, misty droplets clung like fool's gold to his skin.

She nodded, shivering. With the same impulsive intimacy that he'd taken the chocolate from her lips, he took off his bomber jacket and put it around her shoulders.

"Come on. There's nothing more beautiful than the desert in the rain." The twin smile grooves etched his cheeks. It had been a long time since she'd seen them.

Tannis suddenly felt the way the earth feels when the sun touches it after a long rainy spell—warm . . . nourished . . . irrationally happy.

Happy. Wrapped in Dillon's body heat, steeped in the masculine soap and old leather scent, Tannis experienced another of those explosions of hers. Not a small, tender awakening this time, but an eruption that rocked her to her core. It boiled up in her, demanding some kind of release, but since she'd never experienced anything like it before, and didn't know what that release should be, she just let go of a long, shaken breath and followed Dillon into the rain.

Dillon loved the desert when it rained. There were the smells: the scent of thirsty earth and pungent sage, and the wet-hay smell of dried grass. There was the turbulent sky, with the awesome display of elements spread out like some epic battle among the gods. But more than anything, there were the colors. The colors of the desert were muted and subtle; ordinarily the sun bleached them almost to a monochrome in varying shades of ivory, like drying bones. But in the rain the soft pastels became fresh and vibrant, and colors and patterns appeared where there were none before.

"It's like being inside a watercolor painting," Tannis said in a voice that seemed hushed and awed.

Unbidden stirrings of pleasure made Dillon turn and look at her. She had paused on the crest of the hill behind his house and was looking out across the valley. Her chin was lifted and her arms were down at her sides; her face was rain-washed but rapt, the cold forgotten.

He walked slowly back to her, knowing it was dangerous, fully aware that the ache he felt inside himself was the need to take her in his arms.

"Oh, Dillon," she said, turning to him, "I love it here. How did you ever find this beautiful place?"

He cleared his throat. It seemed a safe subject. "I didn't, actually. Logan did."

She smiled. "Logan again. Have the two of you known each other a long time?"

Dillon nodded. "We go back a long way. We were in the academy together, we were rookies together, best man at each other's weddings. That sort of thing. When Logan's first child was born, he decided L.A. wasn't anyplace to raise a kid, so he moved out here. Desert land was cheap then, and he talked me into coming out and taking a look at this 'great opportunity.' Of course I said, 'Yeah, sure, next you'll be selling swampland in Florida, right?' But . . . well, I ended up putting a down payment on the lot without talking it over with Cindy first." His smile was rueful. "Big mistake. She hated the place on sight."

"How could anybody hate this?"

"Well, she was from Seattle. As far as she was concerned, the desert was too hot, too dry, and too empty." He shrugged and looked away, dismissing past disappointments. "The desert's not for everybody, I guess."

"Well, I love it!" Her laughter had a carefree sound, like tumbling water. "There's so much light, and air, and space!" She whirled impulsively away from him, her face lifted to the rain, her arms widespread in a joyful pirouette. "Clarence would *love* this place!"

"Clarence?"

"Yeah, one of the street people I've been studying. He's claustrophobic."

And you understand him, Dillon thought, realizing suddenly that her fear of deep personal involvement was a kind of claustrophobia. That insight and his own urgent need suddenly collided like opposing air masses; the resulting tumult drowned out the voices of reason, blew away his self-control, and blinded him to the consequences of his actions. Emotions of gale force swept through him as he caught Tannis and spun her breathless and laughing into his arms.

Her laughter died as she looked up into his face. Her eyes darkened; her lips parted. For a moment he stood still, feeling the frantic pace of her breathing, feeling his own respirations time themselves to hers. He brought unsteady fingers to her face to brush away the raindrops. And then he lowered his head and took her mouth with all the passion and hunger that was in him.

He kissed her without any restraint at all, hard and deep, giving neither of them time to think or reason. It was a blitz, a tidal wave, a flash flood; it had caught him first, and he meant to sweep her up and carry her along with him if he could.

He knew the moment it happened. He knew the moment the fine, taut thread of her resistance snapped, tumbling her into the vortex that had already claimed him. He heard her whimper, then a sigh in surrender as her arms lifted and her rain-cool fingers touched his face, combed through his hair, and finally clung to the back of his neck.

He made a low sound of wordless approval and fitted his hands to the sides of her waist under her sweatshirt. As he slipped them upward against her skin she gasped at their coolness, opening to him even more. He felt as if he were drowning in her, barely aware that his fingers had fanned over her ribs and back, that his thumbs were brushing the silken undersides of her breasts, following that gentle, weighted curve to slowly circle the pebbled tips. Desire and need became a corkscrewing pain that speared him from chest to groin, so that finally it was he who had to tear his mouth away from her in order to release the screaming pressure in his lungs.

"Dillon!" She said his name as a gasp of shock.

"Oh, Lord," he said, meaning no profanity at all, and caught her against him. Resting his cheek on her hair, he folded his arms around her and felt the turbulence inside her come together with his own in a roiling storm of labored breathing, surging heartbeats, and tight inner trembling.

After a while, when the storm inside him showed no sign of abating, he drew away from her a little and, with one hand framing her face, lifted it so he could look into her eyes. "This time," he said through cramped jaws, "I know for darn sure I meant to do that. Tannis, I . . ." He stopped, swallowing the words that would have voiced his need of her, feeling as if he were swallowing rocks instead.

He needs me, Tannis thought, seeing what was so naked in his face: the deep-etched grooves, the purple smudges, the hunger in his eyes. It was neither the dark side nor the light, but something else, something in shadowed limbo between the two. And she knew suddenly that for this moment at least, she was his sunlight.

Dillon *needed* her. She couldn't remember anyone ever needing her before—really needing her. Oh, many men had spoken plaintively of need when what they'd really meant was want. But here was a man whose need was so great, he couldn't speak of it at all. She felt powerful and humble, joyful, and a little frightened, everything tumbling around inside her until she thought she might explode with it.

"Dillon," she whispered and, laying her hand over his, she held it tenderly against her cheek. And she smiled, offering herself to him, giving to him for no other reason except that it was what she wanted to do.

He searched her eyes, trying to read what he saw there, struggling to believe it. Tannis waited, blinking raindrops, licking them from her lips. And then, at last, with agonizing slowness, still cupping her face in his hand, Dillon lowered his mouth to hers, released his sigh against her parted lips and took the rain from them as if it were an offered blessing.

The kiss was gentle, and the more compelling because of its restraint. She could feel his urgency in his heart's erratic thumping, hear it in the slight harshness of his breathing. She knew it, too, by the way he kissed her with such exquisite, excruciating thoroughness, forcing himself not to hurry, though heat and passion were surging through his body in waves, like seismic shocks.

She was shivering again by the time he lifted his head. He gave her another long look, his own eyes for once unshuttered, the hunger in them stark and unvarnished for her to see. The question was evident in his eyes, too, but it was Tannis who tenderly touched his face and asked, "Why don't we go inside?"

Ten

A cloudburst caught them a hundred yards from the house. They came into the kitchen laughing and stamping water onto the tile floor.

"Oh, wow, look at your jacket," Tannis said breathlessly. "I hope it isn't ruined."

"It'll be fine," Dillon assured her as he slipped it off her shoulders, "but you're soaked."

She turned and placed her hand flat against the front of his sweater. "So are you."

There was the briefest of pauses, and then he said, "Yeah . . . we should probably both get out of these wet clothes." He lifted dripping strands of hair delicately away from her face. In a voice as gentle as his hands he said, "Why don't you go first? Use my bathroom while I see if I can start a fire."

She looked up at him, touching the drops on the end of her nose with the back of her hand. "But . . . you're wetter than I am. Aren't you—"

"I'm fine," he said softly, making a little nudging motion with his hand. "You go on. Take a shower if you like. I think the blue bathrobe's clean."

She gazed at him uncertainly, seeking reassurance, but his eyes had no answers for her; they were soft, but dark and opaque as dead coals.

"Go," he said firmly, taking her by the shoulders and turning her. "Before you're chilled to the bone. Right through there and down the stairs."

She had no choice but to go. As she went through the door she looked back and found him watching her, wearing his smile like a mask. What, she wondered, feeling banished and confused, had happened to the need, to the urgency and the passion in him? Had she only imagined it, or had it taken no more than a dash of cold rain to put out the fires?

Dillon's bedroom was like the living room—vaulted, skylighted ceilings, hardwood floors, soft rugs, muted colors. She entered it like a trespasser, feeling odd about the intimacy of it but unable to keep her eyes from avid explorations.

The room was clean but not neat; clothing hung over the backs of chairs, and the pale fur bedspread had been pulled up over ambiguous bumps and ridges. Neither a neat freak nor a slob, Tannis thought with tender amusement; just a busy man with no time to spare for unnecessary fussing.

In the bathroom she found the Jacuzzi tucked away in a walled atrium with a glass roof to let in sun or starlight. She understood Dillon's slight embarrassment now. The whole thing—the indoor hot tub, skylights, huge furry bed—it all painted a picture that could have borne the caption: California Swinging Bachelor's Pad, 1980s. Funny . . . she'd never thought of Dillon in that light before. Doing so now gave her a queasy feeling.

Throwing off her fears along with her wet clothes, she turned on the hot water and stepped into the shower. She thought about using the Jacuzzi. She thought about how good it would feel to lie back and relax and let herself steep in soothing bubbles. . . .

But hot tubbing wasn't much fun alone.

She didn't stay in the shower long either, just long enough to banish the chill in her body. Then she put on Dillon's blue terry-cloth bathrobe, towel-dried her hair and combed it with her fingers, and returned to the living room.

Dillon was on one knee in front of the sandstone fireplace, gazing contemplatively into the flames. Tannis came upon him quietly in her bare feet, so at first he didn't know she was there.

And, suddenly, she knew what had happened to the hunger and the passion. It was all there, in his unguarded face, in his eyes, even in the lines of his body. Why had he buried it, she wondered. Why was he trying to hide his need from her?

Oh, but it was hard to see him that way, so vulnerable. She thought of other times . . . that day in the park when she had first seen the two sides of Dillon James . . . and again this morning. Why did she feel such a terrible, aching desire to feed and comfort him, to take away the bleakness in his eyes?

Sensing her presence at last, he turned to smile at her. His eyes were soft . . . unreadable.

"Hi," she said, not knowing what else to say.

He stood up and came toward her. "I see you found everything."

She laughed and lifted her arms, draped in the too-long sleeves of his robe. "Yeah, thanks. But . . . um, you're still wet."

"Oh—yeah. Well, I guess the fire's going okay, so . . . I'll go and change. Back in a minute."

He started past her. She moved just slightly, blocking his path. Locking her gaze with his, she put her hands on his hips.

"Tannis . . ."

Without a word she caught the bottom of his sweater in her hands and lifted it. He closed his eyes; she heard the whisper of an escaping breath, and then in one quick movement he hauled the sweater up and over his head.

"Your skin's so cool," she whispered, sliding her hands

up over his ribs. She noted but didn't remark on the narrow silver slashes of old knife scars there. They were just a part of him, like the pattern of dark brown hair on his body, and the cluster of three small moles near the apex of his rib cage.

"Tannis," he said again, hoarsely this time. He covered her wandering hands with his, trapping them against his sides.

For a long moment her gaze didn't waver, and then, with a sigh, she closed her eyes and leaned her forehead on Dillon's chest. Beneath her hands, somewhere deep inside him, she felt him shiver.

His hands gripped her shoulders, hard. "What's the matter?" she whispered against his skin, warming him with her breath.

"I don't know." His voice grated in his chest. "An attack of conscience, I guess."

She gave a soft, shaky laugh. "For what, seducing me? I don't see how you can . . . it looks to me like I'm the one doing the seducing."

He chuckled, a breathy spurt of surprise and amusement. "Oh, is that what you're doing?"

"Yes. I think so. I've never tried it before." It was funny; she felt so calm. Almost . . . sleepy. For the first time she was full of confidence, and the absolute certainty that this was right. "Dillon?" she moved her open mouth back and forth across his chest. "Um . . . I could probably use a little encouragement. Could you please tell me how I'm doing?"

"You know very well how you're doing," he said thickly. His hands had gentled on her shoulders, massaging her through the layers of blue terry cloth. Now they moved slowly downward along the lapels of the robe . . . found and unknotted the sash . . . pulled it away and let it drop. The robe fell open. Reaching inside, his hands sought her waist, spanned it, and drew her to him. Her nakedness cringed pleasantly against his hard, cold body, trembling with shivers of shock and

delight as his hands left her waist and slipped downward again, curving over her bottom, gathering her in.

The unexpected bite of rough fabric against her belly
and the downy softness below made her gasp. His response was immediate and devastating; shifting only a
little, he nudged his thigh between hers, inflaming the
tender flesh there. Heat raced through her body in a
scalding flood and settled, throbbing, in the part of her
that was receiving that insistent pressure. Suddenly
losing the support of her legs, she braced her hands
against Dillon's neck and sagged against him, riding
the hard, vital ridge of his thigh.

As she turned her cheek against his chest and ex-
pelled her breath in a long sigh, she felt him lift her,
criss-crossing her body with his arms, touching her
with blatant eroticism in so many ways, in so many
places. Caressing her bottom, cradling her nape, teasing her sensitized nipples against the raw-silk roughness of hair, tracing the delicate shell of her ear with
his mouth, sending ripples of exquisite sensation shooting along her nerves with every breath.

Her arousal was an explosion, white-hot and devastating, her response to it a small, desperate cry:
"Dillon—"

All of a sudden she wasn't calm and confident anymore. She wasn't a languid seductress taking sensual
pleasure in her own and in her partner's responses.
She was riding a lightning bolt, out of control. And all
of a sudden she knew that her experience with Dan
bore no more resemblance to what was happening to
her now than a cozy fireplace does to a forest fire.

Dillon picked her up and stood for a moment with
her in his arms, looking down into her shock-glazed
eyes. He heard her quick, shallow breaths, and the
little break in them when she swallowed. He felt the
small vibrations in her body, and saw the sheen of
perspiration that dusted the bridge of her nose and the
delicate skin under her eyes. He recognized panic when

he saw it. Tenderness flooded through him, taming his own passions. Smiling, he whispered, "It's all right . . . I've got you."

Her laugh resembled a whimper. Touching his lips with her fingers, she murmured, "Some seducer I am . . ."

His smile formed against her fingertips. "Yeah, you are."

She felt his warm breath, and then a kind of melting as he drew her fingers one by one into his mouth, stroking their sensitive pads until they tingled, and the tingling ran into her palm, up her arm, and then all through her body. She licked her own lips, suddenly wanting the taste of him there. Her hand lay along his jaw, her fingers tracing the outline of his ear while the still-wet tips of his hair touched them like tiny kisses.

Something swelled inside her, like a wave gathering momentum, making her body arch involuntarily toward his. She slid her fingers into his hair and lifted her face, seeking him blindly.

"Tannis"—his breath caressed her parted lips—"I want you. In fact—" There was a sigh, and the lightest of touches, like satin. "I think . . . I really need you." His lips pressed delicately against hers. His tongue drew a tantalizing line along the inside of her lower lip. "But I'll take you home this minute if that's what you want."

"I don't want to go home." She moved her head from side to side, making her open mouth slide against his, finding that warm-slick contact as breathtaking as brandy.

"What do you want?" His voice was a growl she felt deep inside. Her heartbeat was thunderous. She drifted on undulating waves of sound. "I want . . ."

"Yes?"

"I want . . ." She was floating, whirling, caught in a maelstrom of heat and thunder, pulsing rhythms and rapturous spirals. She didn't know whether she said the words, or only formed them in her mind. *I want you.*

. . . She lay on her back on the soft rug before the fire. Dillon's robe was a jumble underneath her, something she barely noticed, and minded not at all. His body was arranged alongside and above hers, making her aware of its hard, rough weight with all of her softest, most sensitive places. One of his hands held one of hers captive, pressed against the rug near her ear. His other arm cradled her head, his hand stroking her throat, lifting her chin, holding her mouth in readiness for him, while her hand clung to the firm, resilient muscle of his shoulder as if to a life preserver.

She looked up at his face and saw the grooves she loved, and her body lifted in a sinuous, unconscious yearning. She closed her eyes, sighed, and then opened the fingers of her captive hand, giving to him the gift of her unconditional trust and surrender.

Languorously now, in the slow, honeyed dance of passion, Dillon laced his fingers with hers. As he lowered his head, breaths hung suspended, then merged in a warm, intoxicating swirl. Lips touched, brushed, and sampled . . . silk on satin . . . then shifted and sampled a new and more erotic melding, while his fingers traced a delicate line along the arch of her throat.

Beneath his fingers Dillon felt the flutter of a pulse . . . a fragile thing, like the struggles of a captive butterfly. And yet, when he pressed his mouth against it, it seemed to echo and rebound through the whole of his being. Overcome, he turned his face into the hollow of her neck. Her hand slipped up over his shoulder to stroke the back of his neck, almost as if she were comforting him.

He felt the quickening rise and fall of her chest, pushing the gentle swell of her breasts against his chest. Pulling back from her a little, he watched the dusky crests change shape and texture, watched the firelight flit across her skin in random patterns of gold and shadows, and thought he'd never seen anything so beautiful. The fire burned hot, searing her breasts and his back like the rays of a midsummer sun; and yet, compared to the scalding need inside him, it felt more like a summer rain. Stunned by his need, and her response to it, he bowed his back and brought his mouth to one tender nipple.

At first he only warmed it with his breath, holding it in his open mouth, teasing, tormenting . . . while she held her breath. Her stomach muscles tightened and trembled beneath his. When at last he touched the pebbled tip with his tongue, drawing gentle, laving circles around it, her breath escaped her in a shuddering gasp, and this time it was her thigh muscles that tightened.

He knew it was only an involuntary tightening, a feminine reflex of protection. Nevertheless, he lifted his head and, catching her free hand, carried it to the rug above her head and held it there. Gently interweaving his fingers with hers, he stared down at the pattern of stress wrinkles in her forehead and whispered, "I can still stop if you want me to. . . ."

"No!" It was a whimper almost of pain.

"Tannis, open your eyes," he commanded hoarsely. "*Look at me.*"

She obeyed him like one coming out of a drugged sleep.

"I'll never hurt you. In *any* way. You know that, don't you?"

She nodded, her drowned eyes clinging to him. He hesitated then, knowing what he was about to ask of her, understanding that there is no one so naked and vulnerable—both physically and emotionally—as a woman when she opens herself to a man. "Trust me," he whispered, knowing that she had trusted a man once and had her trust cruelly violated.

When she sighed, "I do . . ." and he felt her body relax and move sinuously under his, and her thighs open to make a place for him, he was so shaken he forgot about his own nakedness and vulnerability. And he forgot, while he had promised from his heart never to hurt her, that he had neglected to secure the same promise from her in return.

I didn't know, Tannis thought as she exploded . . . heart, soul, and body. It was her last coherent thought for a while. She was used to explosions, but *this* . . . this was holocaust, something she wouldn't survive without being irrevocably changed. From this moment nothing would ever be the same for her again. It was as if the old Tannis had been vaporized and a new one formed from the floating, drifting molecules. . . .

And the difference in her was Dillon. He was with her in the holocaust, a part of it, and ever afterward he would be a part of her; destroyed and reformed into a new whole, not a joining, but a blending.

And yet none of that was conscious thought, only feelings. All she knew, when she was once again fully aware of her body and the one she held so tightly in her arms, was that she never, ever wanted to be separate from him again. *Dillon.* Now he was a real and solid weight on her chest, belly, and thighs, his arms a strong support under her, his back sweat-slick and cool beneath her stroking hands. The melding of their bodies seemed complete—legs entwined, flesh upon flesh, rocking gently to the rhythms of each other's pulsebeats. She felt that to separate herself from him now would be an agony akin to having her heart ripped from her chest.

When he lifted his face from the warm curve of her neck, she actually gave a small cry of pain, and he asked her what was wrong.

"Don't leave me," she whispered, frightened.

His eyes were tender and a little sad. "I won't," he said, not quite understanding. "I told you that."

"No—I mean *now.* Please, stay and hold me a little longer."

"As long as you want me to." He brushed his open mouth across her forehead. "But . . . I must be heavy."

"No!" She hugged him fiercely.

"Oof," he gasped, laughing. "Here . . . I have an idea." Ignoring her protests, he rolled onto his back, bringing her with him, altering their union only slightly. "There now," he murmured, stroking her back as she settled upon his chest with a sigh, "that's better. . . ."

"I didn't know," Tannis said sleepily sometime later.

"Know what, babe?" Dillon's voice was groggy.

"Didn't know it could be like this."

There was a pause. She didn't know what she'd have answered if he'd asked her to explain, so she was glad when he only held her more tightly, his chest expanding as if the feelings inside were too intense for words.

Tannis woke up because she was cold, and found that it was night. The house was dark, the fire only a few settling chunks of charcoal.

"Dillon," she whispered, touching his face.

"What is it, babe?" And then, "Oh . . . Lord. What time is it?"

"I don't know, I can't see. Dillon, I'm cold."

"Yeah, me too. And stiff as a board." He groaned and stirred beneath her. "I'm too old to sleep on the floor."

"Oh, dear," she whispered, contrite. "All this time I've been lying—"

"Shh." He hooked an arm around her neck and pulled her down into his kiss. It was a kiss as warm, generous, and nourishing as the sun. A loving kiss. "You can sleep on top of me anytime. In fact, I may do away with blankets permanently. I just need something softer under me, that's all."

"I should get up." But his hand was drifting over the curve of her bottom, scattering shivers across her skin like snowflakes, dragging heat from deep in the core of her body.

"It's up to you . . ." His voice was a resonant burr at the base of her throat, his mouth a hot, drawing pressure. "I said I'd hold you as long as you want me to."

All the parts of her body so recently sensitized to his touch suddenly awakened to throbbing, pulsing life. She stirred restlessly, moving her body on his in a kind of sensuous seeking. "I want"—she gasped as his hand, pressing hard on the base of her spine, brought her to what she was searching for—"you to hold me a little longer, please."

"Just hold you?"

"No!" It was another gasp, this one high and agonized as with his hands and hard, hot body he applied exquisite pressure to her most sensitive places. Aching now, shuddering, already wanting him with a kind of desperation, she cried, "*Love me.* I mean—make love to me . . . again . . . please."

He caught her to him and, in entering her, brought the holocaust with him, searing, white hot, terrifying, picking up where it had left off, like the melody of an interrupted song.

Above the thunder of its dying echoes she heard him say in a voice hoarse with passion, "Right the first time . . . *I love you.*"

The thrill she felt wasn't pleasure, but unease.

"I see stars," Tannis said. "The rain must have stopped."

They were sitting in the Jacuzzi, soaking away the stiffness in bones and muscles unaccustomed to sleeping on floors . . . and a few other pursuits they'd been engaged in recently.

"Yeah," Dillon said, putting his head back and gazing up at the glass roof of the atrium, "but it's only temporary. One front's moving through, but there's another one right behind it. Should be here by late tomorrow."

"What are you," Tannis said, laughing, "the *Farmer's Almanac*?"

Dillon shrugged and grinned lopsidedly through lazy

curls of steam. "Sorry. Habit. My dad was a building contractor. Construction people and farmers—they live and die by the weather forecasts, you know."

"Really?" Each new thing she learned about him gave her a tiny jolt of joy, like raindrops on an up-turned face.

"Yeah . . . one ill-timed day of rain can throw a construction project weeks off schedule."

"I guess I hadn't thought of that." Growing greedier, she prodded, "Dillon? How come you decided to become a cop instead of a builder?"

He shrugged, looking evasive. "I don't know. I learned the trade, of course. I worked for my dad during summer vacations when I was in high school . . . helped put myself through college. One thing I know for sure—builders sure make more money than cops do!" But his chuckle had a brittle sound, and Tannis couldn't let it go.

"Come on, you must have had a reason. What was it, rebellion?"

He looked surprised. "Rebellion? Against my father, you mean? No. Not that he'd have minded having his son go into the family business, I suppose. But he always made it clear to me that I could do anything I wanted to do."

"And . . . you wanted to be a cop. Why?"

He stirred restlessly in the churning water and mumbled something she couldn't hear. When she asked him, he repeated it, sounding gruff and embarrassed. "I thought I could make a difference." He threw her a hard, black look that softened when it touched her face. "You saw the knife scars?" he asked softly.

She nodded. "I thought you got them—"

"—In the line of duty?" He shook his head. "I got those trying to keep my best friend from stopping a bus with his bare hands. We were seniors in high school. He'd gotten hold of some angel dust—PCP—and he thought he was Superman, I guess."

Dillon was silent, and Tannis didn't try to interrupt his thoughts. After a while he said, "I just . . . wanted to see if I could keep that from happening to somebody else's best friend, I guess. That's why I became a cop."

Tannis understood Dillon's dark side now. He was a man who'd come close enough to the abyss to look into hell . . . and he'd stepped back. What she didn't understand was the vast ache she felt inside when she thought about him. Could it be, she wondered, that this was what *love* was? The unconditional, eternal kind of love? Maybe it was just this—not explosions, simply a desire to *give*, to nourish and comfort, to provide warmth and joy and sunlight, to somehow make the darkness less lonely.

All of a sudden, fear gripped her and squeezed so tightly that for a moment she actually felt sick. *It's too much!* something in her cried out in protest. *I'm not ready! I'm not strong enough!* That kind of love took courage, and commitment. She didn't have time for this—not now, not today! There was still so much she wanted to do.

"Tannis? What is it? What's wrong?"

She managed a ripple of unsteady laughter. "And to think I once accused you of not knowing what the streets were like! So," she said on a bright, desperate note, "did you build this house?"

"Well, some of it. Actually Logan and I did quite a bit of the work ourselves. He designed it—this one and his own—or, rather, he and his wife did. That's why it has such a great kitchen . . . and certain other woman's touches."

"What I want to know is," she teased, "whose idea was the indoor Jacuzzi?"

He laughed and mumbled something about "post-divorce self-indulgence," with a touch of embarrassment Tannis found both endearing and amusing. Reaching for her, he kissed her with a steamy abandon that left her dizzy and weak in the knees.

Torpid, heavy, sated with sensual pleasure, they dragged themselves out of the hot tub and into the kitchen for a meal of microwaved gourmet delights. They laughed and talked and finally made love again, this time in Dillon's great big furry bed, taking all the time in the world. . . .

Afterward, he told her again that he loved her. And after a little while, gently stroking her back, he asked her, "Tannis, why do you do that?"

"Do what?"

"You shiver when I say I love you. Why?"

She whispered, "I don't know. I guess because it scares me."

"Babe, what in the world is so scary about being loved?"

"Not . . . *being* loved. It's"—she drew a shuddering breath—"the loving back that's so hard." But it wasn't what she meant!

He held her tightly. "So don't love me back, then. Just . . . be with me."

Be with me. Being with Dillon was wonderful. Being with him here, in his house, in his bed, in his arms . . . she never wanted to leave. She thought about forever, and the knot in her stomach grew harder, heavier, tighter. Until finally she lay awake, listening to Dillon's sleep sounds while tears trickled into her hair.

Because as she stared up through the vaulted skylight of Dillon's beautiful house and gazed at the changing tapestry of moon and stars and silver-edged clouds in the desert sky, she was seeing endless ranks of picket fences.

Dillon knew the minute he woke up that she was gone. *Gone* gone, not gone to the bathroom, or the kitchen, or for a brisk morning walk. He wasn't sure how he knew. Maybe because of the emptiness and desolation in his heart. And maybe because, in a way, he'd almost been expecting it.

He looked for a note, but the only clue to her departure was a telephone number scrawled on the notepad beside the phone in the kitchen. When he dialed the number, a terse voice said, "Los Padres Yellow Cab—" He hung up, swearing, and buried his face in his hands.

"Have a nice day," the cab driver said as he started to drive off.

Tannis stood on the sidewalk looking after him, brushing at the tears on her cheeks. It was a lovely morning, the kind that feels so fresh and clean it seems almost as if the whole world is newborn, all evils erased, all glorious things possible. Rain still clung to the grass and shrubs in tiny crystalline beads. Puddles reflected roiling pink-tinged clouds and lavender sky; woodsmoke drifted lazily from chimneys, spicing the winter-sharp air. The paper boy, making his morning rounds, stopped to hand her the plastic-wrapped morning edition of the *Daily Bulletin.* He looked a little taken aback by her tear-reddened eyes and uncombed hair, but wished her a brave "Good morning!" just the same.

She knocked on her sister's front door, too lethargic to look for her key or garage door opener. Josh answered her knock, wearing his Masters of the Universe pajamas with the feet in them. When he saw her, his face lit up like the Fourth of July.

"Aunt Tanny! Guess what? I'm gonna have a new baby brother or sister!"

"Oh . . ." Tannis said weakly, and then, looking up into her sister's radiantly teary face, asked, "*Really?*"

Lisa nodded, happily sniffling, and held up the tiny glass vial. Her husband Richard came from behind her to wrap her in his arms.

"Congratulations," Tannis said. "I know how much you've wanted another baby. I'm really happy for you."

"I don't have to share my room if I don't want to," Josh said. "But if I want to I can, but only when he's bigger."

"Room! Oh, gosh, that's right—you'll be needing my room," Tannis said, trying surreptitiously to touch away the remnants of her own tears.

"Oh, heavens, not for ages yet! Tan, don't worry about it—really. You'll be finished with your thesis long before then anyway. There's no hurry."

"Actually," Tannis said, clearing her throat, "I've been thinking that I've done just about all I can here. I only have . . . um, a couple of things to take care of, and then I'll be ready to get out of your hair."

"Oh, no—Tan, we don't want you to do that! You don't have to go yet!"

"Yes, I do. It's time," Tannis said huskily, a little desperately. She hugged her sister and brother-in-law and gave Josh a kiss. "I'm thrilled about your news. It's really . . . great."

She escaped at last to the sanctuary of the shower, thankful for the timely preoccupations that kept her family from noticing that she'd arrived on their doorstep at six o'clock in the morning, rumpled and uncombed, whisker-burned and crying.

Dillon went to his office first. He'd argued with himself all the way into town about the futility of trying to track Tannis down. His impulse was to go straight to her sister's house and bang on her front door until she agreed to face him. But she'd run from him because she was afraid of getting involved, afraid of commitment, afraid of intimacy, afraid of love, and chasing her wasn't going to change that.

On the way to his office he stopped by Logan's, but the chief of police wasn't in yet. Feeling restless and frustrated, he stayed at his own desk long enough to locate the addresses of several women's shelters, and then went out again.

He felt a little guilty about going to the vacant lot to pick up the woman and her kids without Tannis. He knew she'd want to be there. But on the other hand, he told himself angrily, it was her own fault. She was the one who'd pulled that childish flit, running out on both him and her responsibilities!

But halfway to the vacant lot he suddenly uttered the vilest oath of which he was capable and hung an illegal U-turn in the middle of a block.

"Councilman James," said the pretty blond woman who answered Dillon's knock, "what a surprise. Tannis isn't here right now. I'm her sister. You probably don't remember, but I met you at one of your campaign coffee parties. This is my husband, Richard, and . . . this is Josh."

"Councilman," Tannis's brother-in-law said, giving Dillon a look of friendly appraisal as he shook his hand. "Come in, have a cup of coffee."

"Please—just Dillon," he said. "Uh . . . no thanks, I'd love to, but—listen, you don't happen to know where she went, do you?"

Her sister shook her head, smiled ruefully up at her husband, and shrugged. "Who knows? I never know *where* she goes when she dresses up like that. I'm not sure I want to." She shivered.

Dillon felt something cold crawl down his spine. "Dresses . . . like what?"

"Oh, well, *you* know . . . like a bag lady."

The vacant lot was empty. Tannis had searched and called through the weeds and oil drums and rusting car bodies, refusing to accept the fact that the woman and her children weren't there any longer. Now she stood in the middle of it all, feeling as desolate and abandoned as her surroundings.

They were gone. Dillon would never have come for them without her; she knew that. So they had gone away—*run away!*—too frightened after all to trust even her. *All those children,* she thought. Where could they have gone? How would she ever find them again? If only she hadn't waited so long. If only she'd done something sooner. If only she'd gone to Dillon sooner. *Dillon.*

Overhead the storm clouds rolled and tumbled, gathering strength. The new system was moving in, as he'd said it would. *What are you, the Farmer's Almanac?*

She didn't know where to go or what to do next. It occurred to her that she didn't even know where to find Binnie and Clarence, or any of her street friends, for that matter. After yesterday's rain the wash would be full of water, so they wouldn't be down at the culvert. The only thing left for her to do was to search through the skid-row missions, city shelters, and private flophouses until she found someone who knew where they might be.

Tannis sniffed and shuffled down the dingy street, brushing at her cheeks with her tattered gloves. A hostile wind sprang up, swirling trash around her feet and knifing its way inside her coat. She felt cold and wretched, lost and defeated, for the first time in her life truly understanding the utter hopelessness, the despair of the homeless ones. . . .

Eleven

Dillon stood in the vacant lot amid the sticker weeds and broken glass with his shoulders hunched, hands jammed deep in the pockets of his leather jacket.

His first thought had been that Tannis had somehow spirited the woman and her children away. The pain of such a denial of trust was still ricocheting and rebounding through his soul, even though he'd pretty much discarded the idea. He didn't see how she could have had time to get here on foot from her sister's place, and get all those kids packed up and out of the area without him seeing some sign of them. It was a long way to the nearest shelter. No, he was pretty sure not even Tannis would try to move that family alone and on foot.

Somehow, such certainty didn't make him feel much better. The family was gone; Tannis was gone. And for the life of him, right at that moment he couldn't think of anything he could do about either one.

In a sudden explosion of frustration Dillon picked up a beer bottle and hurled it savagely against the side of the abandoned gas station. Then he got into his car and drove slowly and carefully back to City Hall. When he arrived there, he parked and locked his car, then stood for a few moments, looking up at the building's Spanish-style facade.

Funny, he thought, he had the resources of an entire city and police department at his disposal, and yet, when it came to finding the woman he loved, they weren't enough.

Instead of going in, he pocketed his keys, zipped up his jacket against the spitting wind, and started up the street toward the corner of Fifth and Cleveland.

As he walked he got angry all over again. He asked himself why he should try to find her at all. So she could run out on him again? As he'd told himself before, he wasn't a masochist. What he wanted was Tannis in his life . . . or clear out of it. But never, ever again did he want to go through the pain of waking up after a night of loving to find her gone, without a word or any kind of explanation. Why should he give her another chance to take potshots at his heart?

But . . . it was cold, and a new storm was coming in. And no matter how hard he tried not to, he kept seeing her out there, wet and alone, wearing that ridiculous purple hat with the pompon on it. There was no use denying it—he cared about her. Cared, hell. He'd fallen in love with her. And no matter how badly she'd hurt him by running away, he had to be sure she was all right. That was all. He just had to know.

" 'Mornin', Councilman," Gunner called out as Dillon approached the newsstand. "What can I do for you?"

Dillon spun a quarter onto the counter. "I need some information."

"That'll get you a newspaper," Gunner said, nodding at the quarter. "Anything else'll either cost you a lot more or a lot less, depending on what you want to know."

"Seen Tannis this morning?"

"Uh-huh." For a long time Gunner looked at him, measuring him in some indefinable way. Dillon stared back at him. "She was here," Gunner said quietly. His chair pivoted silently toward the door in the side of the stand. "A little while ago. Lookin' for her friends. I couldn't help her much. Between the rain and the cops, street folks are pretty scattered right now." The wheelchair rolled through the door and out onto the rain-speckled sidewalk. Maneuvering quickly and efficiently, Gunner lowered the plywood front of the stand, secured it with a padlock, and tucked the key away in the front pocket of his dark green hooded sweatshirt.

"I'm goin' on my break," he said, squinting up at Dillon. "Councilman, you look like a man who could use a cup of coffee." His dark eyes were compassionate. "On me."

For a moment Dillon hesitated, monitoring the rumblings in his belly with some surprise. He'd thought they were caused by tension, but now that he thought about it, he realized he'd dashed out of the house without shower, shave, or breakfast.

"Sounds good," he said, managing a smile. "Thanks."

Gunner grinned and gave a little jerk of his head. "This way, Councilman." Dillon had to walk briskly to keep up with him.

"Something I've learned," Gunner said over Danish and coffee at Sam's Deli, "and that's you can't keep somebody if they really want to go."

"What gets me," Dillon said, "is that she couldn't trust me." They were talking about the woman with the children in the vacant lot. "What's sad is, she didn't even know there was anybody she could turn to."

Gunner nodded. "Lot of people out there with that problem, Councilman. Just don't know where to go, or who to ask for help. Problem is, they don't trust anybody, most of 'em, and with good reason." He hunched forward, cupping his huge hands around his coffee mug. "See, my friend, it's like this. When you've been out in the cold a long time, it gets hard to come into the warm, because you're scared it's too good to be true. You get to thinkin' it's gonna be just a dream, and you're gonna wake up and find yourself in the cold again. Most street people, they've been burned a few times. It gets hard to trust after a while. Fear—it's a powerful motivator."

Dillon nodded. After a moment he coughed and said painfully, "Well, it's more powerful than love, I guess."

"You're not talkin' about the woman in that vacant lot." Dillon looked up and found Gunner's eyes resting on him. Quiet eyes, ancient and fathomless. "You're talkin' about Tannis."

"I told her I'd never hurt her. She ran anyway."

"My friend, what I said about street people, that goes for anybody who's ever been burned. It's hard to trust again. I've seen a lot of fear. I saw it in her eyes here a while ago."

"She's afraid of me," Dillon said bleakly. "She's afraid of commitment, she's afraid of intimacy—"

"Scary things," Gunner remarked.

Dillon sighed. "Yeah, I suppose so."

"Well, man, there's nothing in the world you can do to change that. You know it, don't you? She's the only one who can."

Dillon's snort was a futile rejection.

"Human beings are pretty amazing," Gunner said with a gentle chuckle, shaking his head. "Now, they say you can do anything if you set your mind to it. It ain't true, of course, and you and I both know it. For starters, I'll tell you three things no human being can do: You can't make another person happy, you can't make a person trust you, and you can't make 'em love you." He took a swallow of coffee and shrugged as if to say, "That's the way it is."

"Yeah," Dillon said heavily, standing up. "I know. Hey, listen, thanks for the coffee."

"You going looking for her?" Gunner asked as he shook Dillon's hand.

"I guess so. I just want to see that she's all right. I have to do that much."

"I understand."

"Gunner? Keep an eye out for her, okay?"

"I'll do that," Gunner said softly. "Take care, Councilman."

Tannis found Binnie in the Red Cross shelter on Twelfth Street. Lying on the sterile cot without her cart or one of her collection of hats, she seemed small and frail, oddly diminished.

"It's my arthritis," Binnie explained apologetically. "Cold and damp gets me every time. Plus, I think I'm catchin' a cold or somethin'." She patted her bony chest. "Just feel kind of poor, you know?"

Tannis nodded.

Binnie's voice dropped to a whisper. "They put my things in a storeroom downstairs. Do you think they'll be all right? Sure wouldn't want anything to happen to my things."

"Well," Tannis said, "if you can't trust the Red Cross . . ."

"Yeah, that's kind of what I thought. You stayin'?" Binnie looked hopeful. "Maybe they got a bed for you too."

Tannis shook her head. "I'm looking for Clarence. You seen him?"

Binnie shrugged dejectedly. "I tried to get him to come with me, but he wouldn't. Poor old Clarence." She thought for a moment. "Tried The Alley?"

"The Alley!" Tannis said, suppressing a shudder as she remembered what had happened—or almost happened—the last time she ventured into that part of the city. She also had to swallow an ache in her throat when she thought about what had happened after that. "He wouldn't go there, would he?" she asked doggedly.

She couldn't think of Dillon now. She couldn't. If she

thought about Dillon, she'd have to remember the way he'd looked this morning, sleeping, and the way she'd felt, leaving him there. If she did that, the love and the longing would overwhelm her, and she'd forget all her goals and ambitions, all the important things she had to do. . . .

Binnie shrugged once more. "Where else could he go?"

"Yeah," Tannis sighed. She thrust her hands into her coat pockets, hunched her shoulders, and turned away.

"Hey," Binnie said, "you ain't goin' lookin' for him in The Alley. You stay away from there. That's a dangerous place."

"I'll be careful. You take care of yourself, now."

Binnie nodded. "They gave me some aspirin for my arthritis. Just wish I had some vitamin C. They don't give you fresh vegetables in this place."

Tannis promised to bring her some oranges, said good-bye, and left the shelter. It was dusk, and a light rain had begun to fall.

From the windy rooftop Dillon watched the dusk come down and the storm come in as lights winked on in the city below. When the first raindrops hit him, he turned up the collar of his jacket and stuck his hands deep in his pockets, but he didn't leave the roof. Not yet.

It was hard, admitting defeat. He'd spent a futile and frustrating afternoon, walking and driving all over the city, checking all the places he knew of where the homeless people might take shelter from the rain and cold. Either Tannis hadn't been there, or he'd just missed her. He'd swung by the newsstand again, too, hoping Gunner might have news of her, but he'd found the stand closed and padlocked. It gave him some comfort to think that Gunner might have closed up early in order to go out looking for Tannis. He wished him luck, but as for himself, the rooftop had been his last resort. He was fresh out of ideas.

Come on, Dillon, give it up.

He could almost hear Gunner's voice saying, "You can't make somebody love you." And Logan's, chiming in, "Hey, man, you don't need this. There must be a million women out there!"

He knew they were both right, but it was hard to accept. Hard to accept the fact that wanting something badly might not be enough. Not this time. He'd been lucky so far, he supposed, in that anything he'd ever wanted badly enough to really try for, he'd won. Women included. Especially women. He'd been in love a few times before Cindy, and interested a few times since. And it had always been so easy. It sure hadn't ever been like this—the hassle, the doubts, worries, fears. The pain.

He didn't know why he was bothering with it. Well, yes, he did, too. He loved Tannis. He hadn't known her long, but he knew he wanted her with him. Now and, as far as he could see, for the rest of his life. But what he wanted wasn't enough. It was just as Gunner had said: You can't make somebody love you.

Life was too short, Dillon told himself angrily. He'd already paid his dues, served his time in hell. He deserved to be loved . . . trusted . . . cherished. And if Tannis didn't have the guts to put her heart on the line for him . . .

The rain came down harder, striking his face like tiny bits of glass. It was a miserable night, and she was out there in it, somewhere. But it was where she'd chosen to be, and there wasn't a thing he could do about it.

As he made his way down the slippery fire escape and walked to his car, cold bitter night settled over the city, and over his heart.

•   •   •

The Alley didn't look so sinister at night, Tannis thought. The hard edges of squalor blurred in the purple darkness. Streetlights made rippling golden patterns on wet pavement and turned the raindrops into swirling clouds of diamond dust. The neon lights on the honkytonks and porno parlors lent an illusion of tawdry warmth to the place, a kind of blousy festiveness that reminded Tannis of the gaudy trappings of a cold-hearted floozy.

She kept to the lighted sidewalks, pausing only to peer into doorways and the shadowy places between buildings, calling out, from time to time, "Clarence, is that you?" or asking, when she recognized a familiar face, if anyone had seen him. Eyes followed her—dispirited eyes, empty eyes, furtive and hostile eyes.

At the entrance to the alley itself she hesitated, staring into the shadows. She wished she had her shopping cart; it had proven an unexpectedly effective weapon as well as both crutch and shield. Without it she felt naked and defenseless. Fear was a constant constriction in her chest and throat.

"Clarence," she called in a ragged whisper, "are you in there?" And then, a little louder, she murmured, "Clarence?"

There were rustlings and stirrings among the anonymous shapes in the alley. A match flared, briefly illuminating a scruffy beard and hollow features. Tannis turned away, preparing to move on.

From out of nowhere, an arm, thin and sinewy as rope, snaked around her neck, choking off air. She had no chance to struggle, no chance to cry out. Her one thought, as she felt herself dragged backward, spun around, slammed hard against rough brick, was that the thing she'd been so often warned about was actually happening. Her emtions rejected it—it simply couldn't be happening. *Not to her!*

The arm across her throat loosened a little. A high, desperate voice croaked, "Gimme your money!"

"*Money?*" Tannis managed to wheeze and shake her head. She felt an absurd impulse to laugh.

"Come on," the voice whined. "I know you got some money stashed away someplace—all you bag ladies do." Rank breath blew past her ear. She heard a muffled sniff. "Where is it, huh? In your shoes? Maybe you got it sewn up in this coat. . . ."

Clawlike hands gripped her and spun her around, and she found herself staring into a dark, desperate face. The man wasn't much bigger than she was, not much larger than a kid, really, but strong, frighteningly strong. He held her pinned against the wall with one forearm. The other hand held something in front of her face, something that caught the light. A knife.

Tannis opened her mouth but couldn't seem to make any sound come out. She shook her head, staring at the knife, hypnotized by it.

"Look, I don't want to hurt you," the man said, sniffing again, rubbing his nose with the back of the hand that held the knife. "I just need some money. I need it real bad. You must have money—I know you do. Just gimme what you got and I won't hurt you."

A junkie, Tannis thought. Who else would be crazy enough or desperate enough to rob a bag lady? And then she remembered, *Dillon warned me.*

"I have only a few dollars," she said truthfully. She always carried enough for a meal or a ride home in case of a real emergency. "It's . . . in my purse."

"Get it."

Still unable to take her eyes from the knife, Tannis licked her lips and mumbled, "It's inside my coat."

The mugger's arms relaxed slightly. The knife wavered. Tannis's heart beat sharp and quick, like a jackhammer.

And then, from somewhere behind came a voice, anxiously calling, "Win? Is that you?"

Tannis gasped, "Clarence?" She'd just caught a movement from the corner of her eye as the mugger, with a look of pure panic, whirled and struck out blindly with the knife. Tannis saw the knife flash once, and then again; she saw Clarence double over and crumple to the ground. This time his name was a scream: *"Clarence!"*

Without stopping to think of consequences, Tannis hurled herself at the mugger and, like a cornered animal, he turned on her. She fought him mindlessly, instinctively throwing up her arms to protect her face and neck, just trying to keep herself between the knife and Clarence's body. She didn't feel the knife, didn't even know when it scored her flesh. She didn't feel anything at all.

"Tannis!" It was a roar, the sound a lion makes before it springs. There was a whooshing sound, a flurry of movement, flashes of steely light.

The mugger abandoned Tannis to face the new threat, but when he saw the huge barrel-chested man bearing down on him in a wheelchair, waving one massive arm in the air like a club, he gave a panic-stricken cry and ran. The knife went skittering off across the rain-slick sidewalk as his footsteps echoed down the dark alley.

"Hey." Gunner's soft voice rumbled. "Hey, sugar, you okay?"

"Yes, but I think he killed Clarence," Tannis said, and began to sob.

Gunner wheeled himself over to where Clarence lay on his side on the cracked pavement. He leaned down to touch the wounded man's neck. "He's alive," he said, straightening. "Bleeding bad." He spun back to Tannis. "How 'bout you? Come here, let me see. . . ."

"Take care of Clarence," Tannis mumbled. "I'm okay."

"The hell you are," Gunner said. She felt his strong arms support her, heard him say, "Hang on, sugar."

And that was the last thing she remembered.

Dillon was about halfway home when he saw the flashing lights in his rearview mirror. Damn, he thought, annoyed with himself for his carelessness. It was speeding, no doubt. He pulled over and stopped, reaching with resignation for his driver's license and registration.

A California highway patrolman in a yellow slicker tapped on his window, and he rolled it down, squinting against the sting of raindrops and the glare of a flashlight.

"Are you Dillon James?"

That's odd, Dillon thought, nodding.

The patrolman waved his ID aside. "Sorry for the inconvenience, sir. The Los Padres P.D. asked us to be on the lookout for you."

A few moments later Dillon was on his way again, this time with red lights and siren escort.

The automatic sensors that operated the sliding doors at the emergency entrance to Sisters of Mercy Hospital weren't fast enough for Dillon. He almost walked through the plate glass.

"Where is she?" he asked tersely, spotting Logan talking to a couple of uniformed officers near the front desk.

Logan came to meet him and put a calming hand on his arm. "It's okay, buddy. They're both in surgery. They'll make it."

"They?"

"Yeah, one of the street people, from the looks of him. All we know is his name's Clarence."

"Oh, yeah. He's a friend of hers." Dillon dragged a hand through his hair. Reaction was setting in, and he was beginning to feel a little bit light-headed. "Logan, tell me what the hell happened here!"

"Junkie with a knife," Logan said with a sigh, steering him toward the waiting room. "Looks like he was trying to get enough out of her for a fix, when the other guy tried to interfere. The junkie went after him, and

Tannis went after the junkie, according to the guy that found 'em. Looks like this guy saved both of 'em. Can you believe that? The man's in a wheelchair!"

"Wheelchair," Dillon muttered, feeling dazed. "Has her family been notified?"

Logan shook his head. "Didn't know who to call. She was unconscious when they brought her in. The guy in the wheelchair's the one who said to call you. When they couldn't get you at home or your office, the officers suggested they call me. That's how I got into it."

"Where is he?" Dillon asked. "The guy in the wheelchair."

"Right in here." Logan pushed open the door to the waiting room. "Insisted on coming in with her."

Gunner had pivoted away from the rain-streaked windows when he heard the door open. Dillon just stood and watched the chair roll toward him. Unable to think of anything to say, he finally mumbled, "Gunner," and stuck out his hand.

Something stirred in Gunner's eyes. "Councilman," he said as he gripped Dillon's hand. "I wish I'd gotten there sooner."

And then Dillon saw the blood on Gunner's clothes, and felt a sudden and most uncoplike need to sit down.

He'd been through this so many times before, and it had never felt like this, Dillon thought as he stared down at the still, white face amid the usual tangle of tubes and wires. Her face was unmarked, thank God. According to Gunner, she'd instinctively put up her arms to protect it. And her coat—that great big ridiculous coat—had helped to protect her arms. Though they lay on top of the blankets in a mummy wrap of bandages, the doctors had assured him the cuts were superficial. The coat had undoubtedly saved her life. That fact struck Dillon as ironic.

They'd cleaned the latex and makeup from her face.

Asleep, she looked about ten years old. Unable to help himself, Dillon reached out and brushed her cheek with the backs of his fingers, then drew his thumb across the bridge of her nose.

No, he'd never felt this way before, not even with his father's final heart attack. He hadn't felt the fear, or the guilt. He felt responsible. *He* was the reason Tannis was lying here hooked up to IV drips and electronic monitors. He'd moved too fast, pushed her too hard. She'd gone off in a panic, running from her feelings for him, and in such a vulnerable state she'd forgotten to be careful. She'd forgotten the instincts for self-preservation that had landed him in the gutter that very first day. It seemed like a year ago to him now.

"Babe, I'm sorry," he whispered, then turned away.

Back in the waiting room, he found Binnie waiting with Gunner. When Dillon came into the room, she stood up nervously clutching a plastic umbrella with both hands. She was wearing a red beret.

"How is she?" It sounded like she had a bad chest cold. "How's Win?"

"Win?" Dillon glanced at Gunner. "You mean Tannis? She's still sleeping."

"Tannis?"

"That's her name," Dillon said gently. "Tannis Winter."

"No kiddin'? Huh. Well, I don't want to bother her, and, anyway, I have this little cold . . ." Binnie leaned closer to Dillon, peering up into his face. She looked puzzled. "Well, anyway, I heard about what happened. Just wanted to see if she was okay. How's Clarence?"

"He's going to be all right. They both are, Binnie."

She started, frowning. "How'd you know my name? Do I know you?" And then she drew herself up and said with pride, "Bernice MacFadden, that's my name."

"Miss MacFadden," Dillon said, touching her arm. "I'll tell Tannis you were here."

"That's *Mrs.* MacFadden," Binnie said fiercely, lifting her umbrella. "I had a husband once. Had a home of my own when he was alive. Kept it neat as a pin too." She turned away with a defiant lift of her chin. As she went through the door, Dillon heard her add, "And a vegetable garden. Grew the best vegetables in the whole neighborhood. . . ."

Dillon stared after her, looking thoughtful. Gunner came rolling over to him.

"Found her folks yet?"

Dillon shook his head. "Still trying to track down her sister. The baby-sitter says they went out to celebrate. I don't know what they're celebrating, but I guess they'll be back eventually." He rubbed his neck tiredly.

"Somebody better tell the doctors about Clarence," Gunner said mildly. "They're gonna want to sedate him when he comes to, I'd imagine."

"Good point. I'll go tell them." Dillon started out the door, then hesitated and turned back. "You really care about these people, don't you?"

Gunner shrugged. "I been there, Councilman. I do what I can."

"Ever thought about doing more?"

"Maybe." Gunner's eyes were guarded, watchful. "What are you thinkin', Councilman?"

"Ever thought about going back to school?"

"Thought about it. I have my G.I. money. Just never hit on what I wanted to study."

"City College has a good paralegal program. Good handicapped facilities too."

"That a fact?"

"Yeah. I believe I've figured out what I want to do with my own law degree. And I think I could use a partner."

Gunner jerked his head toward the dark windows. "Helping them?" Dillon nodded. "Ain't much money in it," Gunner observed.

Dillon shrugged. "That's true."

Gunner grin[...]
Councilman."

Tannis emerged [...]
Dillon holding her h[...]
and found that talking [...]
Dillon chuckled. "No, [...]
throat hurt too. "You're [...]
scarred up, maybe."

"Matched set," Tannis sa[...]
"He's going to be fine too. [...]
"Oh," Tannis said, sudde[...] [...]e sting of
inexplicable tears. "My throat [...]
"You've had a tube in it. Here, have a sip of water."
She felt the blessed coolness on her lips and in her
throat, and then the warmth of his fingers, brushing
a tear from her cheek. She murmured, "Dillon . . ."
"Your sister's been here. She's called your mom
and dad. They'll be here soon." She heard the scrape
of a chair as he stood up.
"Dillon—" Frustrated tears squeezed between her
lashes and ran into her hair. She wanted his hands
on her face again, but she didn't know how to tell
him.
"Shh, don't cry," he said, sounding torn. "I'm sorry
this happened to you. It shouldn't have happened. I
shouldn't have pushed you so hard. I shouldn't have
told you I loved you. I knew you weren't ready to
hear it."
"Dillon—"
"Tannis, I want you to know I'm not going to bother
you again. So you don't have any reason to run or
hide. My loving you isn't doing either of us any good.
In fact, it's caused us both a whole lot of pain. So . . .
I'm getting out of your hair. I'm going now. You get
some rest . . . get well. And if you ever figure out

, well . . . you know where

. . . me once more, but it was only a
. . . osing door. Incredibly, unbelievably,
. . . she finally understood how much she
. . . im, he was gone.
. . . en she woke up again, soft, cool hands were
stroking her forehead. She sighed and said, "Dillon?" But the voice that answered was her mother's.

"Mom," Tannis said, crying again, "why am I being
so stupid?" Crying seemed to come very easily. Something about being hurt, she supposed; her defenses
were shot to pieces.

She was in a private room, with a television set
instead of electronic monitors. All the tubes were gone
except for the IV in her right arm. She and her mother
were alone—her father had gone to the cafeteria for
coffee—and she'd just told her all about Dillon.

Her mother, a slim and attractive sixty-year-old,
smiled and patted her hand. "You're not being stupid, darling. You're just being . . . you."

Tannis groaned. "Well, that's sure a comfort."

"What I mean is," her mother said, "that you always feel things so hard. Joys and sorrows, highs
and lows—you experience it all with such intensity.
But it's what makes you so special."

"That's a mother thing to say," Tannis whispered.
"What it really makes me is an emotional cripple. I
mean, think about it. Love makes me panic. What
am I supposed to do? Mom, I love Dillon. I really do.
And that terrifies me, even now, even after . . . what
happened." She stopped, feeling breathless and
exhausted.

"Love is one of the most powerful emotions there
is," her mother said matter-of-factly. "And you are a
person who weeps over 'reach out and touch someone' commercials. Of course it's overwhelming."

"What am I going to do?"

"Well, darling, it isn't going to go away, is it?"

Tannis shook her head and sniffed. "No."

"Then, I guess you'll just have to learn to live with it, won't you?"

So simple and so obvious. Tannis thought about it and felt calmer and quieter inside. After a while she stirred and said, "Mom? It isn't just the intensity that scares me. It's the limitations."

"Limitations?" Jan Winter frowned, the watermark of wrinkles more deeply etched in her forehead than in her daughter's. "I don't know what you mean."

"You know—the whole marriage and motherhood thing. Kids, P.T.A., the white picket fence . . . Mom, that's not for me."

Her mother looked surprised. "Well, no, I suppose not."

"But isn't that what it's all about? Love, commitment . . . marriage. And all the rest."

"Darling, that's what it was all about for *me*, because that was what I wanted—and so did your father. It's the love and commitment—and marriage, I suppose—that's important. What you do with it beyond that is up to you, and, of course, to the one you love. It's kind of important you both want the same thing." She leaned over and brushed tears from Tannis's cheeks, making her think again of Dillon. "By the way, how does *Dillon* feel about picket fences?"

"I don't know," Tannis said, staring at her.

"Well," her mother said gently, "don't you think you should ask him?"

The new wooden plaque on Dillon's office door read: D. E. JAMES.

I really must remember to ask him what the *E* stands for, Tannis thought as she pulled the sleeves of her sweater down over the healing knife-wounds on her arms, lifted her hand, and knocked.

Dillon's voice called, "Come in," and she felt that familiar upsurge in her stomach.

He was standing behind his desk just as he'd been the first time she'd ever seen him in this office. Only this time he wasn't smiling. His cheeks looked drawn and his eyes were shadowed, but it wasn't the dark side of him she saw now, just vulnerability and a certain wariness. For the first time Tannis knew how much she had hurt him by running out on him, and she almost lost her courage completely.

"It's good to see you," Dillon said softly, then cleared his throat. "Uh . . . how are you doing? You're looking well."

But I'm not *doing* well at all. I miss you terribly. "Yes, I'm . . . doing fine. Most of the stitches are out now."

"Good . . . good. How's Clarence?"

Tannis gave a one-shouldered shrug. "He's all right. They've transferred him to the state hospital, but he's on medication, and they say the prognosis is pretty good."

"Well, I'm glad to hear that. So . . . what can I do for you?" Dillon looked pointedly at the large box under Tannis's arm. She shifted it so it was mostly behind her.

What can you do for me? Forgive me? "Um . . . I've been looking for Binnie. I asked Gunner, and he said she has a new home, and that you'd know where I can find her."

Dillon finally smiled then, the wide, bracketed smile she loved. The squeezing sensation in her chest almost stopped her heart.

"That's right. Here, I'll give you her address." He sat down at his desk and, taking a pen from his shirt pocket, scribbled rapidly on a memo pad. "There you go," he said, tearing off the sheet and handing it to her.

Tannis glanced at it, then did a double take. "But . . . isn't this—Dillon, this is—"

"My place. Yes. Binnie's my housekeeper now." He grinned. "She's not a bad cook, if you like vegetables. She's already making plans to put in a garden."

"Oh," Tannis said weakly, sinking into a chair.

"Is that something for Binnie?" Dillon asked, nodding toward the box. "I can take it to her if you'd like." His voice and his manner were distant, polite.

"No," Tannis mumbled, feeling heartsick and defeated. "It's for you." She put the box on his desk and pushed it toward him. He gave her an intrigued look.

"For me?"

She nodded and watched numbly as he untied the string and lifted the lid. Dryness settled in her throat as she watched his hands fold back tissue paper and touch the dingy purple pompon, the limp gray wig. She thought, *It's too late. I've hurt him too badly.*

After what seemed like an eternity he looked at her and asked sharply, "What's this for?"

"I don't need it anymore."

He frowned. "You've finished your work, then?"

"No." She shook her head. "I still have a lot of work to do. I've just decided that I don't need the disguise anymore."

"Why are you giving this to me?"

Panic began to stir in her. This wasn't going well at all. She didn't know how to tell him that she was done with hiding and running away, and she was pretty sure it wasn't going to make any difference anyhow. "I just . . . wanted you to know," she muttered, standing up and turning blindly away.

"Tannis." Something about the set of her shoulders reminded him of the way she'd looked that day in the park, walking away from him, trying not to cry. He pushed back his chair, opened his desk drawer, and took out a dirty blue Dodger cap. When she turned to look at him, he was turning it over and over in his hands.

"Have you seen this?" he asked, laying the hat beside

the purple pompon and picking up the newspaper that was lying on his desktop.

The *Daily Bulletin*'s headline read: JAMES SELECTED TO HEAD MAYOR'S HOMELESS TASKFORCE.

Looking puzzled, Tannis stared at it and shook her head.

Dillon took a deep breath. "I still need a partner," he heard himself say. And then, knowing the risk he was taking, knowing he was probably crazy, he went around his desk and gently took her by the arms. Holding himself together, holding her with his eyes, he said harshly, "Tannis, why did you come here? Why did you bring me this? What are you trying to tell me with all this?"

"I—" She stopped, frozen.

He wanted to shake her, shout at her. Instead, he took her ice-cold hands in his big warm ones and said softly, insistently, "Tell me. In plain English, please. What does this mean?"

She swallowed and whispered, "It's hard." Her eyes stared up at him, winter-bright with pain . . . and something else. With love.

"I know," he said as the tension ebbed, and he felt a rush of tenderness. "But it gets easier with practice."

"I . . . love you," she said, then closed her eyes.

"There now," Dillon said softly. "That wasn't so bad, was it?"

She was shaking. "I feel like I just fell off a building."

His voice was tender. "Say it again, so you'll feel more comfortable with it."

"I love you."

"And . . . ?"

"And I'm not going to run out on you ever again."

"Promise?"

"Promise. Oh, Dillon—"

"I want to hold you," Dillon said huskily, "but I don't know where you're hurt."

"My ribs," Tannis said with a broken laugh. "Just

like yours. Now we really are a matched set. But hold me anyway, please. I need you."

I need you. Needing someone, she discovered as Dillon drew her into his arms, was as wonderful, in a different way, as being needed. It felt good to be vulnerable, and to be surrounded by tender, loving arms.

"I have just one question," she said as he bent to kiss her. "How do you feel about picket fences?"

"Picket fences?" He paused, looking bewildered.

Tannis looked up into Dillon's eyes and felt the biggest, most wonderful explosion she'd ever known in her life. An explosion of love and joy and certainty.

"Never mind," she whispered, touching the twin grooves in his cheeks with tenderness. Because suddenly she knew, with all her heart and soul, that it was going to be all right.

THE EDITOR'S CORNER

Next month's LOVESWEPTs are sure to keep you warm as the first crisp winds of autumn nip the air! Rarely do our six books for the month have a common theme, but it just so happens our October group of LOVESWEPTs all deal with characters who must come to terms with their pasts in order to learn to love from the heart again.

In **RENEGADE,** LOVESWEPT #282, Judy Gill reunites a pair of lovers who have so many reasons for staying together, but who are pulled apart by old hurts. (Both have emotional scars that haven't yet healed.) When Jacqueline Train and Renny Knight struck a deal two years earlier, neither one expected their love to flourish in a marriage that had been purely a practical arrangement. And when Renny returns to claim her, Jacqueline is filled with panic . . . and sudden hope. But with tenderness, compassion, and overwhelming love Renny teaches her that the magic they'd created before was only a prelude to their real and enduring happiness.

LOVESWEPT #283, **ON WINGS OF FLAME,** is Gail Douglas's first published romance and one that is sure to establish her as a winner in the genre. When Jed Brannen offers Kelly Flynn the job of immortalizing his uncle's beloved pet in stained glass, she knows it's just a ploy on Jed's part. He's desperate to rekindle the romance that he'd walked away from years before. He'd been her Indiana Jones, roaming the globe in search of danger, and she'd almost managed to banish the memory of his tender caresses—until he returns in search of the only woman he's ever loved. Kelly's wounded pride makes her hold back from forgiving him, but every time she runs from him, she stumbles and falls . . . right into his arms.

Fayrene Preston brings you a jewel of a book in **EMERALD SUNSHINE,** LOVESWEPT #284. Too dazzled by the bright blue Dallas sky to keep her mind on the road, heroine Kathy Broderick rides her bike smack into Paul Garth's sleek limousine! The condition of her mangled bike isn't nearly as important to Kathy, however, as the condition of her heart when Paul offers her his help—

(continued)

and then his love. But resisting this man and the passionate hunger she feels for him, she finds, is as futile as pedaling backward. Paul has a few dark secrets he doesn't know how to share with Kathy. But as in all her romances, Fayrene brings these two troubled people together in a joyous union that won't fail to touch your soul.

TUCKER BOONE, LOVESWEPT #285, is Joan Elliott Pickart at her best! Alison Murdock has her work cut out for her as a lawyer who finds delivering Tucker's inheritance—an English butler—no small task. Swearing he's no gentleman, Tucker decides to uncover Alison's playful side—a side of herself she'd buried long ago under ambition and determination. Alison almost doesn't stop to consider what rugged, handsome Tucker Boone is doing to her orderly life, until talk of the future makes her remember the past—and her vow to rise to the top of her profession. Luckily Tucker convinces her that reaching new heights in his arms is the most important goal of all!

Kay Hooper has written the romance you've all been waiting for! In **SHADES OF GRAY,** LOVESWEPT #286, Kay tells the love story of the charismatic island ruler, Andres Sereno, first introduced in **RAFFERTY'S WIFE** last November. Sara Marsh finds that loving the man who'd abducted her to keep her safe from his enemies is something as elemental to her as breathing. But when Sara sees the violent side of Andres, she can't reconcile it with the sensitive, exquisitely passionate man she knows him to be. Andres realizes that loving Sara fuels the goodness in him, fills him with urgent need. And Sara can't control the force of her love for Andres any more than he can stop himself from doing what must be done to save his island of Kadeira. Suddenly she learns that nothing appears black and white to her anymore. She can see only shades of gray . . . and all the hues of love.

Following her debut as a LOVESWEPT author with her book **DIVINE DESIGN,** published in June, Mary Kay McComas is back on the scene with her second book for us, **OBSESSION,** LOVESWEPT #287. A powerful tale of a woman overcoming the injustices of her past with the help of a man who knows her more intimately than

(continued)

any other person on earth—before he even meets her—
Mary Kay weaves an emotional web of romance and
desire. Esther Brite is known to the world as a famous
songwriter, one half of a the husband and wife team that
brought music into the lives of millions. But when her
husband and son are killed in a car accident, Esther
returns to her hometown, where she'd once been shunned,
searching for answers to questions she isn't sure she
wants to ask. Doctor Dan Jacobey has reasons of his
own for seeking sanctuary in the town of Bellewood—the
one place where he could feel close to the woman he'd
become obsessed with—Esther Brite. Esther and Dan
discover that together they are not afraid to face the
demons of the past and promise each other a beautiful
tomorrow.

I think you're going to savor and enjoy each of the
books next month as if you were feasting on a gourmet
six-course meal!

Bon appetite!

Carolyn Nichols

Carolyn Nichols
  Editor

LOVESWEPT
Bantam Books
666 Fifth Avenue
New York, NY 10103

THE HOMETOWN HUNK CONTEST

FOR EVERY WOMAN WHO HAS EVER SAID—
"I know a man who looks just like the hero of this book"
—HAVE WE GOT A CONTEST FOR YOU!

To help celebrate our fifth year of publishing LOVESWEPT we are having a fabulous, fun-filled event called THE HOMETOWN HUNK contest. We are going to reissue six classic early titles by six of your favorite authors.

DARLING OBSTACLES by Barbara Boswell
IN A CLASS BY ITSELF by Sandra Brown
C.J.'S FATE by Kay Hooper
THE LADY AND THE UNICORN by Iris Johansen
CHARADE by Joan Elliott Pickart
FOR THE LOVE OF SAMI by Fayrene Preston

Here, as in the backs of all July, August, and September 1988 LOVESWEPTS you will find "cover notes" just like the ones we prepare at Bantam as the background for our art director to create our covers. These notes will describe the hero and heroine, give a teaser on the plot, and suggest a scene for the cover. Your part in the contest will be to see if a great looking local man—or men, if your hometown is so blessed—fits our description of one of the heroes of the six books we will reissue.

THE HOMETOWN HUNK who is selected (one for each of the six titles) will be flown to New York via United Airlines and will stay at the Loews Summit Hotel—the ideal hotel for business or pleasure in midtown Manhattan—for two nights. All travel arrangements made by Reliable Travel International, Incorporated. He will be the model for the new cover of the book which will be released in mid-1989. The six people who send in the winning photos of their HOMETOWN HUNK will receive a pre-selected assortment of LOVESWEPT books free for one year. Please see the Official Rules above the Official Entry Form for full details and restrictions.

We can't wait to start judging those pictures! Oh, and you must let the man you've chosen know that you're entering him in the contest. After all, if he wins he'll have to come to New York.

Have fun. Here's your chance to get the cover-lover of your dreams!

Carolyn Nichols

Carolyn Nichols
Editor
LOVESWEPT
Bantam Books
666 Fifth Avenue
New York, NY 10102–0023

THE HOMETOWN HUNK CONTEST

DARLING OBSTACLES
(Originally Published as LOVESWEPT #95)
By Barbara Boswell

COVER NOTES

The Characters:

Hero:
GREG WILDER's gorgeous body and "to-die-for" good looks haven't hurt him in the dating department, but when most women discover he's a widower with four kids, they head for the hills! Greg has the hard, muscular build of an athlete, and his light brown hair, which he wears neatly parted on the side, is streaked blond by the sun. Add to that his aquamarine blue eyes that sparkle when he laughs, and his sensual mouth and generous lower lip, and you're probably wondering what woman in her right mind wouldn't want Greg's strong, capable surgeon's hands working their magic on her—kids or no kids!

Personality Traits:
An acclaimed neurosurgeon, Greg Wilder is a celebrity of sorts in the planned community of Woodland, Maryland. Authoritative, debonair, self-confident, his reputation for engaging in one casual relationship after another almost overshadows his prowess as a doctor. In reality, Greg dates more out of necessity than anything else, since he has to attend one social function after another. He considers most of the events boring, and wishes he could spend more time with his children. But his profession is a difficult and demanding one—and being both father and mother to four kids isn't any less so. A thoughtful, generous, sometimes befuddled father, Greg tries to do it all. Cerebral, he uses his intellect and skill rather than physical strength to win his victories. However, he never expected to come up against one Mary Magdalene May!

Heroine:
MARY MAGDALENE MAY, called Maggie by her friends, is the thirty-two-year-old mother of three children. She has shoulder-length auburn hair, and green eyes that shout her Irish heritage. With high cheekbones and an upturned nose covered with a smattering of freckles, Maggie thinks of herself more as the girl-next-door type. Certainly, she believes, she could never be one of Greg Wilder's beautiful escorts.

Setting: The small town of Woodland, Maryland

The Story:
Surgeon Greg Wilder wanted to court the feisty and beautiful widow who'd been caring for his four kids, but she just wouldn't let him past her doorstep! Sure that his interest was only casual, and that he preferred more sophisticated women, Maggie May vowed to keep Greg at arm's length. But he wouldn't take no for an answer. And once he'd crashed through her defenses and pulled her into his arms, he was tireless—and reckless—in his campaign to win her over. Maggie had found it tough enough to resist one determined doctor; now he threatened to call in his kids and hers as reinforcements—seven rowdy snags to romance!

Cover scene:
As if romancing Maggie weren't hard enough, Greg can't seem to find time to spend with her without their children around. Stealing a private moment on the stairs in Maggie's house, Greg and Maggie embrace. She is standing one step above him, but she still has to look up at him to see into his eyes. Greg's hands are on her hips, and her hands are resting on his shoulders. Maggie is wearing a very sheer, short pink nightgown, and Greg has on wheat-colored jeans and a navy and yellow striped rugby shirt. Do they have time to kiss?

THE HOMETOWN HUNK CONTEST

IN A CLASS BY ITSELF
(Originally Published as LOVESWEPT #66)
By Sandra Brown

COVER NOTES

The Characters:

Hero:
LOGAN WEBSTER would have no trouble posing for a
Scandinavian travel poster. His wheat-colored hair always
seems to be tousled, defying attempts to control it, and
falls across his wide forehead. Thick eyebrows one shade
darker than his hair accentuate his crystal blue eyes. He
has a slender nose that flairs slightly over a mouth that
testifies to both sensitivity and strength. The faint lines
around his eyes and alongside his mouth give the impression that reaching the ripe age of 30 wasn't all fun and
games for him. Logan's square, determined jaw is punctu-
ated by a vertical cleft. His broad shoulders and narrow
waist add to his tall, lean appearance.

Personality traits:
Logan Webster has had to scrape and save and fight for
everything he's gotten. Born into a poor farm family, he
was driven to succeed and overcome his "wrong side of
the tracks" image. His businesses include cattle, real estate, and natural gas. Now a pillar of the community,
Logan's life has been a true rags-to-riches story. Only
Sandra Brown's own words can describe why he is masculinity epitomized: "Logan had 'the walk,' that saddle-
tramp saunter that was inherent to native Texan men,
passed down through generations of cowboys. It was, without even trying to be, sexy. The unconscious roll of the
hips, the slow strut, the flexed knees, the slouching stance,
the deceptive laziness that hid a latent aggressiveness."
Wow! And not only does he have "the walk," but he's fun

and generous and kind. Even with his wealth, he feels at home living in his small hometown with simple, hard-working, middle-class, backbone-of-America folks. A born leader, people automatically gravitate toward him.

Heroine:

DANI QUINN is a sophisticated twenty-eight-year-old woman. Dainty, her body compact, she is utterly feminine. Dani's pale, lustrous hair is moonlight and honey spun together, and because it is very straight, she usually wears it in a chignon. With golden eyes to match her golden hair, Dani is the one woman Logan hasn't been able to get off his mind for the ten years they've been apart.

Setting: Primarily on Logan's ranch in East Texas.

The Story:

Ten years had passed since Dani Quinn had graduated from high school in the small Texas town, ten years since the night her elopement with Logan Webster had ended in disaster. Now Dani approached her tenth reunion with uncertainty. Logan would be there . . . Logan, the only man who'd ever made her shiver with desire and need, but would she have the courage to face the fury in his eyes? She couldn't defend herself against his anger and hurt—to do so would demand she reveal the secret sorrow she shared with no one. Logan's touch had made her his so long ago. Could he reach past the pain to make her his for all time?

Cover Scene:

It's sunset, and Logan and Dani are standing beside the swimming pool on his ranch, embracing. The pool is surrounded by semitropical plants and lush flower beds. In the distance, acres of rolling pasture land resembling a green lake undulate into dense, piney woods. Dani is wearing a strapless, peacock blue bikini and sandals with leather ties that wrap around her ankles. Her hair is straight and loose, falling to the middle of her back. Logan has on a light-colored pair of corduroy shorts and a short-sleeved designer knit shirt in a pale shade of yellow.

THE HOMETOWN HUNK CONTEST

C.J.'S FATE
(Originally Published as LOVESWEPT #32)
By Kay Hooper

COVER NOTES

The Characters:

Hero:
FATE WESTON easily could have walked straight off an Indian reservation. His raven black hair and strong, well-molded features testify to his heritage. But somewhere along the line genetics threw Fate a curve—his eyes are the deepest, darkest blue imaginable! Above those blue eyes are dark slanted eyebrows, and fanning out from those eyes are faint laugh lines—the only sign of the fact that he's thirty-four years old. Tall, Fate moves with easy, loose-limbed grace. Although he isn't an athlete, Fate takes very good care of himself, and it shows in his strong physique. Striking at first glance and fascinating with each succeeding glance, the serious expressions on his face make him look older than his years, but with one smile he looks boyish again.

Personality traits:
Fate possesses a keen sense of humor. His heavy-lidded, intelligent eyes are capable of concealment, but there is a shrewdness in them that reveals the man hadn't needed college or a law degree to be considered intelligent. The set of his head tells you that he is proud—perhaps even a bit arrogant. He is attractive and perfectly well aware of that fact. Unconventional, paradoxical, tender, silly, lusty, gentle, comical, serious, absurd, and endearing are all words that come to mind when you think of Fate. He is not ashamed to be everything a man can be. A defense attorney by profession, one can detect a bit of frustrated actor in his character. More than anything else, though, it's the

impression of humor about him—reinforced by the elusive dimple in his cheek—that makes Fate Weston a scrumptious hero!

Heroine:
C.J. ADAMS is a twenty-six-year-old research librarian. Unaware of her own attractiveness, C.J. tends to play down her pixylike figure and tawny gold eyes. But once she meets Fate, she no longer feels that her short, burnished copper curls and the sprinkling of freckles on her nose make her unappealing. He brings out the vixen in her, and changes the smart, bookish woman who professed to have no interest in men into the beautiful, sexy woman she really was all along. Now, if only he could get her to tell him what C.J. stands for!

Setting: Ski lodge in Aspen, Colorado

The Story:
C.J. Adams had been teased enough about her seeming lack of interest in the opposite sex. On a ski trip with her five best friends, she impulsively embraced a handsome stranger, pretending they were secret lovers—and the delighted lawyer who joined in her impetuous charade seized the moment to deepen the kiss. Astonished at his reaction, C.J. tried to nip their romance in the bud—but found herself nipping at his neck instead! She had met her match in a man who could answer her witty remarks with clever ripostes of his own, and a lover whose caresses aroused in her a passionate need she'd never suspected that she could feel. Had destiny somehow tossed them together?

Cover Scene:
C.J. and Fate virtually have the ski slopes to themselves early one morning, and they take advantage of it! Frolicking in a snow drift, Fate is covering C.J. with snow—and kisses! They are flushed from the cold weather and from the excitement of being in love. C.J. is wearing a sky-blue, one-piece, tight-fitting ski outfit that zips down the front. Fate is wearing a navy blue parka and matching ski pants.

THE HOMETOWN HUNK CONTEST

THE LADY AND THE UNICORN
(Originally Published as LOVESWEPT #29)
By Iris Johansen

COVER NOTES

The Characters:

Hero:
Not classically handsome, RAFE SANTINE's blunt, craggy
features reinforce the quality of overpowering virility about
him. He has wide, Slavic cheekbones and a bold, thrusting chin, which give the impression of strength and authority. Thick black eyebrows are set over piercing dark
eyes. He wears his heavy, dark hair long. His large frame
measures in at almost six feet four inches, and it's hard to
believe that a man with such brawny shoulders and strong
thighs could exhibit the pantherlike grace which charac-
terizes Rafe's movements. Rafe Santine is definitely a man
to be reckoned with, and heroine Janna Cannon does just
that!

Personality traits:
Our hero is a man who radiates an aura of power and
danger, and women find him intriguing and irresistible.
Rafe Santine is a self-made billionaire at the age of thirty-
eight. Almost entirely self-educated, he left school at six-
teen to work on his first construction job, and by the time
he was twenty-three, he owned the company. From there
he branched out into real estate, computers, and oil. Rafe
reportedly changes mistresses as often as he changes shirts.
His reputation for ruthless brilliance has been earned over
years of fighting to the top of the economic ladder from
the slums of New York. His gruff manner and hard personality hide the tender, vulnerable side of him. Rafe also
possesses an insatiable thirst for knowledge that is a
passion with him. Oddly enough, he has a wry sense of

humor that surfaces unexpectedly from time to time. And, though cynical to the extreme, he never lets his natural skepticism interfere with his innate sense of justice.

Heroine:

JANNA CANNON, a game warden for a small wildlife preserve, is a very dedicated lady. She is tall at five feet nine inches and carries herself in a stately way. Her long hair is dark brown and is usually twisted into a single thick braid in back. Of course, Rafe never lets her keep her hair braided when they make love! Janna is one quarter Cherokee Indian by heritage, and she possesses the dark eyes and skin of her ancestors.

Setting: Rafe's estate in Carmel, California

The Story:

Janna Cannon scaled the high walls of Rafe Santine's private estate, afraid of nothing and determined to appeal to the powerful man who could save her beloved animal preserve. She bewitched his guard dogs, then cast a spell of enchantment over him as well. Janna's profound grace, her caring nature, made the tough and proud Rafe grow mercurial in her presence. She offered him a gift he'd never risked reaching out for before—but could he trust his own emotions enough to open himself to her love?

Cover Scene:

In the gazebo overlooking the rugged cliffs at the edge of the Pacific Ocean, Rafe and Janna share a passionate moment together. The gazebo is made of redwood and the interior is small and cozy. Scarlet cushions cover the benches, and matching scarlet curtains hang from the eaves, caught back by tasseled sashes to permit the sea breeze to whip through the enclosure. Rafe is wearing black suede pants and a charcoal gray crew-neck sweater. Janna is wearing a safari-style khaki shirt-and-slacks outfit and suede desert boots. They embrace against the breathtaking backdrop of wild, crashing, white-crested waves pounding the rocks and cliffs below.

THE HOMETOWN HUNK CONTEST

CHARADE
(Originally Published as LOVESWEPT #74)
By Joan Elliott Pickart

COVER NOTES

The Characters:

Hero:
The phrase tall, dark, and handsome was coined to describe TENNES WHITNEY. His coal black hair reaches past his collar in back, and his fathomless steel gray eyes are framed by the kind of thick, dark lashes that a woman would kill to have. Darkly tanned, Tennes has a straight nose and a square chin, with—you guessed it!—a Kirk Douglas cleft. Tennes oozes masculinity and virility. He's a handsome son-of-a-gun!

Personality traits:
A shrewd, ruthless business tycoon, Tennes is a man of strength and principle. He's perfected the art of buying floundering companies and turning them around financially, then selling them at a profit. He possesses a sixth sense about business—in short, he's a winner! But there are two sides to his personality. Always in cool command, Tennes, who fears no man or challenge, is rendered emotionally vulnerable when faced with his elderly aunt's illness. His deep devotion to the woman who raised him clearly casts him as a warm, compassionate guy—not at all like the tough-as-nails executive image he presents. Leave it to heroine Whitney Jordan to discover the real man behind the complicated enigma.

Heroine:
WHITNEY JORDAN's russet-colored hair floats past her shoulders in glorious waves. Her emerald green eyes, full breasts, and long, slender legs—not to mention her peaches-

and-cream complexion—make her eye-poppingly attractive. How can Tennes resist the twenty-six-year-old beauty? And how can Whitney consider becoming serious with him? If their romance flourishes, she may end up being Whitney Whitney!

Setting: Los Angeles, California

The Story:
One moment writer Whitney Jordan was strolling the aisles of McNeil's Department Store, plotting the untimely demise of a soap opera heartthrob; the next, she was nearly knocked over by a real-life stunner who implored her to be his fiancée! The ailing little gray-haired aunt who'd raised him had one final wish, he said—to see her dear nephew Tennes married to the wonderful girl he'd described in his letters . . . only that girl hadn't existed—until now! Tennes promised the masquerade would last only through lunch, but Whitney gave such an inspired performance that Aunt Olive refused to let her go. And what began as a playful romantic deception grew more breathlessly real by the minute. . . .

Cover Scene:
Whitney's living room is bright and cheerful. The gray carpeting and blue sofa with green and blue throw pillows gives the apartment a cool but welcoming appearance. Sitting on the sofa next to Tennes, Whitney is wearing a black crepe dress that is simply cut but stunning. It is cut low over her breasts and held at the shoulders by thin straps. The skirt falls to her knees in soft folds and the bodice is nipped in at the waist with a matching belt. She has on black high heels, but prefers not to wear any jewelry to spoil the simplicity of the dress. Tennes is dressed in a black suit with a white silk shirt and a deep red tie.

THE HOMETOWN HUNK CONTEST

FOR THE LOVE OF SAMI
(Originally Published as LOVESWEPT #34)
By Fayrene Preston

COVER NOTES

Hero:
DANIEL PARKER-ST. JAMES is every woman's dream come true. With glossy black hair and warm, reassuring blue eyes, he makes our heroine melt with just a glance. Daniel's lean face is chiseled into assertive planes. His lips are full and firmly sculptured, and his chin has the determined and arrogant thrust to it only a man who's sure of himself can carry off. Daniel has a lot in common with Clark Kent. Both wear glasses, and when Daniel removes them to make love to Sami, she thinks he really is Superman!

Personality traits:
Daniel Parker-St. James is one of the Twin Cities' most respected attorneys. He's always in the news, either in the society columns with his latest society lady, or on the front page with his headline cases. He's brilliant and takes on only the toughest cases—usually those that involve millions of dollars. Daniel has a reputation for being a deadly opponent in the courtroom. Because he's from a socially prominent family and is a Harvard graduate, it's expected that he'll run for the Senate one day. Distinguished-looking and always distinctively dressed—he's fastidious about his appearance—Daniel gives off an unassailable air of authority and absolute control.

Heroine:
SAMUELINA (SAMI) ADKINSON is secretly a wealthy heiress. No one would guess. She lives in a converted warehouse loft, dresses to suit no one but herself, and dabbles in the creative arts. Sami is twenty-six years old, with

long, honey-colored hair. She wears soft, wispy bangs and has very thick brown lashes framing her golden eyes. Of medium height, Sami has to look up to gaze into Daniel's deep blue eyes.

Setting: St. Paul, Minnesota

The Story:
Unpredictable heiress Sami Adkinson had endeared herself to the most surprising people—from the bag ladies in the park she protected . . . to the mobster who appointed himself her guardian . . . to her exasperated but loving friends. Then Sami was arrested while demonstrating to save baby seals, and it took powerful attorney Daniel Parker-St. James to bail her out. Daniel was smitten, soon cherishing Sami and protecting her from her night fears. Sami reveled in his love—and resisted it too. And holding on to Sami, Daniel discovered, was like trying to hug quicksilver. . . .

Cover Scene:
The interior of Daniel's house is very grand and supremely formal, the decor sophisticated, refined, and quietly tasteful, just like Daniel himself. Rich traditional fabrics cover plush oversized custom sofas and Regency wing chairs. Queen Anne furniture is mixed with Chippendale and is subtly complemented with Oriental accent pieces. In the library, floor-to-ceiling bookcases filled with rare books provide the backdrop for Sami and Daniel's embrace. Sami is wearing a gold satin sheath gown. The dress has a high neckline, but in back is cut provocatively to the waist. Her jewels are exquisite. The necklace is made up of clusters of flowers created by large, flawless diamonds. From every cluster a huge, perfectly matched teardrop emerald hangs. The earrings are composed of an even larger flower cluster, and an equally huge teardrop-shaped emerald hangs from each one. Daniel is wearing a classic, elegant tuxedo.